They Are Ruining Ibiza

A. C. Greene

Also by A. C. Greene

A Personal Country
Living Texas
The Last Captive
The Santa Claus Bank Robbery
Dallas: The Deciding Years
A Christmas Tree
Views in Texas
A Place Called Dallas
Elephants in Your Mailbox (with Roger Horchow)
The 50 Best Books on Texas
The Highland Park Woman
Dallas USA
A Town Called Cedar Springs
Texas Sketches
It's Been Fun
Taking Heart
900 Miles on the Butterfield Trail
Joy to the World
Christmas Memories

They Are Ruining Ibiza

A. C. Greene

University of North Texas Press

Denton, Texas

©1998, A. C. Greene

All rights reserved
Printed in the United States of America
First edition

5 4 3 2 1

The paper in this book meets the minimum requirements of the American National Standard for Permanence of Paper for Printed Library Materials, Z39.48.1984.

Permissions
University of North Texas Press
PO Box 311336
Denton TX 76203-1336
940-565-2142

Library of Congress Cataloging-in-Publication Data

Greene, A. C., 1923–
They are ruining Ibiza / by A.C. Greene.
   p.   cm.
ISBN 1-57441-042-3
I. title.
PS3557.R3795T48 1998
813'.54—dc21   97-39440
                                            CIP

Illustrations by Geoffrey Greene
Design by Betty Tomboulian

This is for Geoffrey and Arabella,

the beloved ones who introduced me to Ibiza.

One

As the plane left the Madrid airport, Charles Martyn, PhD, age sixty-two, author of *A Last Look at the American Novel*—used (as a reviewer of the third edition noted) "in virtually every North American college or university where the department chair has not written a similar, but inferior, book"—told Susan, his second wife, that the first thing they would see when they landed on the island of Ibiza would be windmills.

"They are the chief characteristic of the island," he said.

"Like Dutch windmills?" Susan asked.

"Nothing at all like Dutch windmills," Charles said.

"I mean, *characteristic* of the place, the way Dutch windmills are of Holland."

"Dutch windmills have become mere symbols; these are in use," he said.

"Oh, pardon me, then," Susan said, with a slight shrug. She turned and looked out the plane's window, watching the land, then the sea, below. Charles realized she was miffed but, damn it, he could not bring himself to apologize for such an insignificant bruise. He tried reading the Spanish newspaper the attendant had passed out—most of the other passengers appeared to be Spanish—but found he lacked the concentration necessary to decipher a foreign language. He watched Susan out of the corner of his eye as he read, or pretended to read, and when it seemed to him that the shadow had left her face, he took her hand and said, "*Una peseta por sus pensamientos.*"

She looked at him and frowned, "One *peseta?* What was the exchange rate at the airport?"

"It was one-fifty, plus."

"One-fifty to the dollar . . . so you're not even offering me a penny for what I assume are my thoughts?"

"I will raise the offer to *tres pesetas*, which is a great deal more than a penny for your thoughts."

"A great deal more? What, penny-and-a-half? Two cents?"

They Are Ruining Ibiza

"Damn it, you know I'm not a numbers person. It's the thought that counts."

"It's *my* thoughts that count. But, since you did so generously raise your offer, and I know how difficult such decisions are for you to make, I accept. Give me the two cents."

"It will have to be in *pesetas*. I changed all my American money back at the Madrid *Internacional*."

"That's fine; when in Spain do as the Spanish do, I've always heard."

"But the smallest coin I got at the exchange was a five-peseta piece."

"That's all right. I'll take it."

"But that's two more *pesetas* than I offered you."

Susan grabbed the coin Charles held. "I owe you two *pesetas*."

"Well, then . . . tell me your thoughts, please."

She sighed, "You are selfishly inclined, darling. Lovably, but selfishly. Other than musing as to why you are, I was wondering if the people in the villages and on the boats below us give a thought to this airplane as it passes over them . . . a plane full of other people who think being aboard this plane is the most important thing in the world."

"I must say, under the circumstance involved, I agree with the latter sentiment," Charles said. She turned to the window again.

"Well, don't you?" he asked.

3

She replied without looking back, "I suppose so."

A few minutes later the female flight attendant asked, in halting English, if they wished a drink. Charles refused for both of them.

"You didn't want any of their liquor did you, Susan? There's no way seventy proof gin can be used to construct a decent martini."

She turned away from the window. "What about brandy? Isn't Spain famous for brandy?"

"The only decent liquor served aboard European aircraft is vodka, and only because decent vodka is cheap."

"Thank you for being so thoughtful of my liver, or whatever is disturbed by those inferior drinks."

"For God's sake, Susan . . . I'll call her back and get you some Spanish brandy. I turned down the drinks because I was certain you wouldn't like them."

"Never mind. I'm sure you're right. I'm sure that anything they might serve is abominable."

Still mad, Charles thought to himself, as if it were *his* fault that European airlines didn't offer decent drinks.

He studied the other passengers. There was a group of carefully dressed Spanish men in tailored suits, wearing beautiful shoes of Spanish leather. Everything they had on matched. They seemed to be professionals of some sort, all carrying briefcases. He pointed the men out to Susan, who said she had noticed them.

"That one, the white-haired señor, is rather dashing," she said.

They Are Ruining Ibiza

Charles suggested, in a low voice (he was sure several of them spoke English), that, in this jet age, they were commuters who fled the sophistication of Madrid for the simplicity of Ibiza on weekends, the way New York editors fled to the Hamptons.

"In that case," Susan whispered, "the Spanish commuters seem to be going in the wrong direction, because this is Monday."

A Spanish girl and her obviously wealthy mother carried a large, gaudily decorated Mexican *charro* hat in a plastic wrapper. When a flight attendant offered to put it in the rack above them, the girl refused. The hat was so large it covered the laps of both women. It seemed strange to Charles that an elegant Spanish lady, going to Ibiza, should display no more taste than some middle-class American tourist on a package tour of Mexico. And the hat was probably made in Taiwan.

Damn Susan for being so stubborn and pretending she was still mad. Once he turned to her and said, "I'd feel a lot better if we'd heard from Ledyard . . . if he'd answered our cablegram."

"Cablegrams," Susan said. "You sent two." Apparently she did not intend engaging in more conversation. And, apparently, she was going to pass all the blame to him for anything that went wrong on this trip.

❈❈❈❈

A. C. Greene

My God, my God . . . Ibiza, those years ago, when he and Harriet and young Led had been here: The dozens of uninhabited beaches, the quiet villages and little inns, narrow roads through the dusty green hills, the *calles* in D'alt Vila, the old "high" town that rose up to the sixteenth-century fortress; where you could touch the whitewashed houses on either side of the passageways with your outstretched arms. He remembered the old Ibicenco women in black, head to foot, and younger ones in starched, bunched skirts and raised bodices which caused them to look pregnant—made that way initially as protection against the Barbary pirates, someone told him. Mediterranean pirates, those eons ago, might rape pregnant women but found them unhandy to sell as slaves. Ibiza . . . Ibiza: there was the little museum with its lovely, ancient pieces dedicated to Tanit, the Carthagenian goddess of love; there was that bit of rock in the sea where the Ibicencos believe Hannibal of Carthage was born, and the interior villages, still a century or two behind the world. What a lovely, remote time that had been. The visit was ruined, of course, eventually. Everything he had done was ruined eventually . . . except Susan. Harriet had gone from his life, their marriage an overcome calamity—no, that was unfair to both of them; a drama that lost its intensity, being sat through too many times in rehearsal. And the end had started on Ibiza.

They'd sat outdoors most of that night, drinking *café con leche* at a dockside bar in Ciudad Ibiza. Ledyard,

They Are Ruining Ibiza

sunburned and tired, had gone to his room at the hotel. The waiter asked them over and over if they wanted *veeskee borbon o escoses*, very proud that he understood American drinking habits. He lurked in the shadows, waiting. It bothered him that they wanted only Spanish coffee and hot, steamed milk.

Harriet, not much given to lecturing, had lectured her husband. "Why can't you just be human," she asked, "at least to your wife and child? You don't have to be loving and tender. Neither of us any longer expects that. Just be decent."

"You can't speak for Led. He's old enough to know what he thinks about his father."

"I don't need to speak for Led. If you had a few grains of fatherly sensitivity you would know for yourself. You've pushed him to the back of your life. I've been there for years, but he can't understand it."

The memory was still keen. The whitewashed town rising behind them asleep, a few lights around the harbor where they sat, quiet Mediterranean sounds washing across them. It should have been the most glorious night they'd spent together, not even matched by their wedding night. But as he listened to Harriet, to the night sounds, he warned himself that this was serious, that this was not one of those repetitive, bantering quarrels he often promoted, or seldom tried to end. There was a finality to her voice and her words that was urgent and unfamiliar. She had been thinking these things for a long time, building toward a decision.

That dark, dockside night, as they sat in bitter silence, Charles had wavered, his emotions swinging back and forth. He remembered how much he had loved her, those first years, and had wanted nothing from life but her companionship, her aid and abetting. Had he changed too much—or had she not changed enough? He had almost taken her hand, almost asked her forgiveness for being the way he was . . . but it was already impossible, even then. He was too proud of that reputation: Martyn never cracks. And he discovered also, despising himself as he did, that there was a tiny thrill growing, an anticipation of the disaster they were near. He loved her, he supposed. Yes, he loved Harriet . . . but the magnetism of danger was stronger even than that; the attraction to recklessness, the urge to push the moment to a crisis and let it slide over the edge, carrying them with it. After that night, he knew it would certainly end. And it did.

❊❊❊❊

The plane banked over the Mediterranean, approaching Ibiza. The southern end of the island moved, uncomfortably, back and forth across the horizon as the pilot lined up the plane for its descent.

Pointing out the slanting window, Charles informed Susan, "Those are the salterns. *Ses salines*, the Ibicencos

They Are Ruining Ibiza

call them, in the island's Catalan dialect. Salt is evaporated out of sea water in the salt pans. They've been doing it since the time of the Phoenicians."

"Charles, don't you ever get tired of knowing so much?" Susan asked.

He did not acknowledge her question. "Salt is Ibiza's major industry," he continued.

Susan smiled. "I thought drugs—or was it topless beaches?—were Ibiza's major industry." Again, he did not answer.

"Charles, can I go topless on Ibiza?" She waited, obviously offering an armistice. "Charles?"

He was looking at the Spanish tabloid. A full-page photograph showed a variety of sunbathing females on a beach, most of them displaying their breasts. She must have seen him looking at the photograph. He turned the page quickly.

"*May* I go topless, Charles?" she repeated. When he would not answer she nudged him.

"You're too old to go topless," he said, still looking at the newspaper.

"I'm not as old as you are," she said.

He put down the newspaper. "You're thirty-seven years old and that is a bit old to go topless on Ibiza or anywhere else."

She made a face, "I'm not thirty-seven, I'm thirty-six." She cupped her breasts, "And I'm thirty-six here, too."

He glanced down the plane's aisle to see if anyone had noticed his wife's movement. "I don't care how admirable your bosom may be, it's too old . . . I mean, thirty-six is too old to go topless on the beach."

"But you'll go topless . . ."

He turned back to the Spanish newspaper with a frown of annoyance. He had rather enjoyed the beach photograph at which she had caught him looking.

"Stop acting like a child," he told her. "You're a woman, not a man."

"Oh, so that's the reason . . . not my age but my gender. That's sexism."

He pushed the newspaper into his lap and looked at her. "Are you trying to provoke a quarrel?"

She smiled, "I'm trying to provoke a laugh, Charles. You've been far too somber."

"Why don't you study Ibiza and not worry about my risibilities?" He was still hoping he could turn back to the photograph.

Susan mused, "Charles, you pronounce 'Ibiza' as though it were spelled with a 'th' instead of a 'z.' Is there some secret of Spanish grammar . . ."

"Diction," Charles interrupted.

"Well, grammar, diction . . . what is it?"

"It's no secret," Charles leaned back in his seat. "It's Castilian Spanish, the literary language of Spain. The Castilian lisps the soft 'ess' and 'cee' sounds and they become 'th.'"

They Are Ruining Ibiza

"Just a local peculiarity, then," Susan said.

"No, indeed. It has a historical antecedent. Some Spanish king—probably a Ferdinand or an Alfonso, there were dozens of them—lisped, and the court, to avoid him embarrassment or to curry favor, began lisping and it became fashionable—and persists today in Spain as standard Castilian; though not in North and South America."

Susan shrugged. "Dumb me. I had to ask."

"Nothing dumb about it," Charles assured her. "I'm glad you did."

"I was not serious, dear. I was amused at your scholarly explanation."

The plane descended and began its long taxi to the terminal. Charles had told Susan not to be shocked by the terminal building, that its flat tin roof and stucco construction were typical of Ibiza. But as they came out of the rear door of the plane he saw that the terminal was nothing at all as he remembered. The building was surprisingly large and displayed the international design that made every airport look like every other airport.

"There have been changes," he told Susan, as they hurried toward the gate. "The charm is gone. Utterly gone."

"Oh, I thought that automobile graveyard alongside the runway was rather charming. I saw all sorts of quaint vehicles."

At the baggage claim area a green-lettered sign lighted up, giving their flight number. The carrousel began to clank and groan, then to discharge a series of bags. Charles reached across the moving belt and grabbed for Susan's familiar yellow leather shoulder bag (which she had checked against his advice), but he no sooner touched it than another hand grasped its handle and a tall Spaniard with a mustache said to him, "*Con perdon, señor.*" For one moment Charles refused to release the bag, but then, with considerable chagrin, saw that it bore a tag with Spanish wording and, even more embarrassing (as Susan's bag emerged almost immediately after), saw that the Spaniard's was of infinitely better quality and unquestionably of greater cost. The owner of the other must have believed he was trying to steal it. Charles said, gesturing toward Susan's approaching bag, "*Yo confundo el . . .*" (what the hell was the Spanish word for bag? Satchel?) ". . . *con el suyo.*" Now that he had Susan's, the two bags looked nothing alike.

"Think nothing of it," the Spaniard said, in excellent English but with a coolness Charles took for disbelief. Charles went about the job of securing the remainder of their baggage with wrathful concentration.

Several other passengers had four-wheel carts for their luggage and Susan, looking at the pile theirs made, asked, "Why don't you get us one of those carts . . . or let me get one while you find Ledyard and Christy?"

"You have no idea what those luggage carts rent for. Remember, we're fair game. We've got *turista americana* written all over us."

They Are Ruining Ibiza

"It doesn't look to me like they cost anything. Everybody's getting one. Maybe a few *pesetas*."

"They may lease them by the month. Those are commuters."

"Good heavens, Charles, you can't always know . . . They're tourists, just like we are . . . but it's too late now. The carts are all gone."

They took their luggage to the exit where an armed, uniformed man stood. He didn't demand to be shown the baggage claim checks but Charles showed him theirs anyway. The man peered at the numbered stubs and asked, "*Que?*" Charles pointed to their luggage and said to the man, "*Estas son nuestros* (that goddamn word again) . . . *bolsas!*"

The uniformed man smiled and said, "*Vd. tiene buen ojo.*"

Charles and Susan took up their bags and Charles said, "*Mil gracias,*" and the man, still smiling, shrugged, "*Por nada.*"

"What was all that?" Susan asked.

"He was saying he trusted us, I think."

The tall Spaniard, behind them now, smiled at Charles. "He said you showed foresight, bringing luggage." He walked away, holding the expensive yellow leather bag.

Susan giggled. "Who's your new friend?"

"A damned arrogant bastard who thought I was trying to steal his goddamn bag, a while ago," Charles told her.

"Arrogant? He seemed polite."

"He pretended he didn't speak English until I made a fool of myself in Spanish, then he almost purred, his accent was so smooth."

"Oh, that's pretty damned arrogant, all right, speaking English," Susan said.

Charles set the bags down. "Look . . . go find Led and Christy and let's forego further native encounters."

"Certainly. Although you'd think I could recognize a bastard, after all these years."

Two

Susan left him with the pile of baggage while she went out the front gate to see if Ledyard and his wife had arrived to pick them up. Charles watched the crowd, thinking to himself they looked very much the same as a bunch of people around a baggage carrousel at LaGuardia or O'Hare. "There are no more natives," he told himself. "The world is populated with the same nomadic tribe, its members just speak local dialects." He liked the thought and decided to write it down, thinking it would come in handy next time the *Times* wanted an Op-Ed piece from him. But a quick exploration of his coat pockets reminded him he had nothing to make a note on or with. He wished he had remembered to include a small notepad with his passport and wallet. Or a pen. Why was it he never had an inspiration when he was equipped to capture its fleeting moment? Maybe if he had brought the little laptop computer Susan had given him on their anniversary . . . but he hated the idea that people would see him operating the thing and think, aha, there's a guy pretending he's an author.

God, he hated the "Who are you?" tribe that went around cornering people they thought might shed a little of their fame on them with an autograph. "I do textbooks, madam," he once told a glittery bitch in the lobby of Alice Tully Hall during book awards night when she marched up and asked if he was an author. "Then you haven't written any real books I might have read?" the silly bitch asked, and he told her, "No, I am obliged to write for people who can think and read at the same time." It was a stupid answer to a stupid question. Indeed, he too sometimes wondered why he didn't write *real* books; books about infamous people, and sex, and the disastrous political and economic directions the world was taking, pushing and dragging its culture with it. How ironic that his most successful work had predicted the demise of real books, as that silly woman called them.

Susan came back to where he waited.

They Are Ruining Ibiza

"I'm afraid, darling, we're going to have to get a hotel room or find a taxi driver who is able to find Led's place. He and Christy simply are not out there."

"Guard the bags, " Charles commanded. "I'll find him."

❊❊❊❊

Although the sun was still in sight, the shadows were growing longer as they stood watching vehicles picking up and discharging passengers. "I think we'd better get a hotel room," Susan said again.

"Hotels are no problem on Ibiza," he assured her, "and Christy and Led will get here. Christy will see to it. She's more dependable than my son."

Susan walked back inside the terminal and in a few minutes returned. "I talked to the woman who is in charge of the reservations desk. She says we may have difficulty getting a room tonight."

"Nonsense."

"She knows what she's talking about, Charles. The hotel association hires her to book rooms for tourists. This is the height of the season."

"Nonsense. They don't need a hotel association on Ibiza. And the tourist season was over three weeks ago. She's shilling for some resort. Let her get us a room and we'll end up paying three hundred bucks a night."

A. C. Greene

Susan's face was tight, "All right, Dr. Martyn, you find a hotel room."

He frowned back at her. "Don't get on your high horse, just because I happen to know a little something about this island. If we can't locate Ledyard we'll get a room around the airport, or go into Ciudad Ibiza. It's just a chip shot from here. Worse comes to worse, there are native *pensiones* the taxi drivers know about."

"I've had my say. But if I don't have a room and a hot bath tonight you are going to have one furious wife on your hands, dear Dr. Martyn."

Charles flagged one of the taxis that stood in a rank and talked to the driver when it pulled up. In a moment he came back to where Susan stood with the bags.

"Your friendly airport shill may have our necks in her noose," he told Susan. "The taxi driver, as near as I could ascertain, wouldn't, or couldn't tell me about hotel rooms or Led's address."

"Did you draw that conclusion from his English or your Spanish?"

"I drew it from the driver. 'No' is pretty much the same in any language."

"In other words, you found out you are completely wrong and that whatever you think you remember about this island is out of date." She motioned toward the terminal building. "I'm going in and book a room. You may join me if you wish." She turned and went inside. Charles followed.

They Are Ruining Ibiza

❋❋❋

He looked at the receipt in his hand. "Santa Eulalia? . . . why Santa Eulalia when we're right here in the suburbs of Ciudad Ibiza?"

"I told you, hotel rooms are hard to find right now." Susan grinned, "Besides, it's only a chip shot up the island."

"Leaving the visitor at the mercy of the merciless taxi drivers," Charles said. "I wonder how much she padded this bill?"

"I don't care. At least we'll have a roof over our heads. Besides, I think if you will do a little mental arithmetic you will discover the price, whatever it is, comes to about a third of what a room in New York or Boston might run. Here, let me see it."

He shook his head. "You forget, I have a calculator on my wristwatch." He smiled. "First time I've ever found a real use for the damn thing." He pulled back his coat sleeve and punched in a series of numbers on the tiny face of his watch. He inspected the result. "It comes to . . . $38. I hope that's per night, not per person."

"And you think she's shilling for some resort? I hope to God she is, at that rate. Now, get us a taxi."

"But . . . shouldn't we give Led and Christy a little more time?"

"Oh, my God, you are the hardest-headed son of a bitch I've ever known. Led and Christy aren't coming.

A. C. Greene

That's pretty plain by now. At least, it's plain to me. We've been waiting almost two hours. Something may have happened to keep them from getting here or, who knows . . . they may not have gotten our cables. A nice young woman at the tourist information desk told me, in what I considered good English, that the address you have for Led, where you sent the cablegrams, *estanco* San Lorenzo, is a tobacco store. The Spanish equivalent of a 7-Eleven. He probably never got either of them. You want to go to the San Lorenzo 7-Eleven at midnight and ask for your son?"

"You certainly seem to have acquired a wealth of knowledge about the island of Ibiza in the short time you've been on it."

"If you weren't so damn hard-headed . . . " then she smiled, and tiptoed to kiss his cheek. "I'm sorry I called you a son of a bitch, darling. You know I didn't mean it. But the young lady at the information desk is from San Lorenzo. She should know."

"Does she know Led and Christy?" Charles was wiping lipstick from his cheek.

"No. She says San Lorenzo is more a region than a town."

Charles frowned. "Damn Led. He knew we were coming."

"He may not. My informant says the *estanco* is very informal. He and Christy may not have picked up their mail."

They Are Ruining Ibiza

"But on Ibiza . . . a place as small as this island . . . I thought everyone would know him by now."

Susan smiled, "Ah, you finally admit you made a mistake; you presumed something which was irrational."

"It was rational from my experience. You forget, I've been here before."

"How could I forget, with you telling me every five minutes. But you have not been here . . . not *this* Ibiza. You said so yourself, coming into the airport. Everything has changed including the people who live here."

Charles picked up two bags, "Yes, and goddamn it, I can already see, they're ruining Ibiza." He looked annoyed. "Let's hope we can get a cab that will make the trip to Santa Eulalia in one piece. The taxis here are notorious, not to mention the fares."

"The taxis look new, to me. And the girl at the reservations desk told me the fares are regulated and listed. The tourist bureau 'protects the strangers,' her very words."

Charles snorted, "I'll bet . . . and who's going to protect the strangers from the tourist bureau? Every guidebook I've ever read insists a traveler ask the fare *first*, then trust to the tourist bureau and its regulated figures."

There were several taxis lined up, all appearing to be reasonably clean. "There's a new Fiat," Charles said. "I'd like to take it, but it's for guests of one of the resorts up on the north end of the island, some four-star place like La Hazienda."

A. C. Greene

"It looks like a regular taxi to me," Susan said. She motioned to the line and the automobile Charles had been talking about, a black vehicle with a broad red horizontal stripe around the body, pulled to where they were, and the driver stepped out of the car. "Is this a taxi?" Charles asked. "*Sí, señor,*" the driver said. He was a young man with strong white teeth which he displayed with every word.

"Would it be possible for us to be taken . . ." Charles started saying, then saw the young driver did not understand his English.

"Why don't you just show him the receipt . . . the hotel receipt?" Susan asked.

"Because I'm damn sure going to know what the fare is before I hop in that cab," Charles told her. He turned to the driver.

"*Cuantos . . . precio . . . al hotel . . .*" he turned to Susan. "What the hell's the name of that fleabag you booked us into?"

"Show him the receipt. I can't pronounce the name. It's Catalan, I think."

"*Cuantos a . . . aquí?*" Charles stuck the receipt in the driver's hand. The driver looked at the receipt, smiled again, and said, "*Sí, 'otel Ses Estaques. Mil seiscientas pesetas.*"

"*En ingles, por favor, señor?*" Susan smiled at the young man. The driver smiled at her, and bowed, "*Pues bien,*" he took his finger and traced the figure "1600" in the dust of

They Are Ruining Ibiza

the cab's trunk. He produced a printed card from his shirt pocket and ran the same finger to a line of type, "*Aquí . . . Ses Estaques en Santa Eulalia. Mil seiscientas pesetas.*"

Susan turned to Charles, "Well, you understood that, I suppose? Your Spanish is a thousand percent better than mine. Sixteen hundred pesetas to hotel *Ses Estaques* in Santa Eulalia. That seems to be the regulated fare . . . at least, it says that on that card." She motioned toward the vehicle, "Providing, of course, this notorious taxi can get there in one piece."

Charles read the receipt again. "Ask him what *Ses Estaques* means. It may mean flophouse, in colloquial terms."

"Oh, Charles, for God's sake. It's a topnotch hotel, the girl told me."

"And we *must* take the girl's word for everything, mustn't we?"

"Well, I might point out, she's been a lot more accurate than you . . ." Susan paused. "Give her credit for that."

The driver, smiling, said to Charles, "*Ses Estaques, 'sta bueno.*"

"We'll worry about the quality after we arrive," Susan said. "I'm getting in the cab. You can join me or not as you please."

"I have to find a place for all this luggage," Charles said. But the driver smiled and reached for the bags.

"H'okay, señor," he said, "h'okay you get in." He opened the trunk and began expertly inserting the bags.

Charles got into the rear seat with Susan. "You win," he said tightly, "you and the airport shills," but he finally gave a weary grin. "Damn. I was hoping I could hear the Spanish word for suitcase. It's been bothering me ever since we arrived."

"I heard him," she said. "It's *maleta*."

"*Maleta*? When did you hear him say *maleta*?"

"Is it or is it not the Spanish word for suitcase?"

"I guess *maleta* is okay . . . but it's not the word I remembered."

Susan patted Charles on the arm, "I'll see to it, darling, that these mean old Spaniards ask your permission before they use unfamiliar words."

There was still faint daylight remaining when the taxi left the airport and started through the outskirts of the capital, Ciudad Ibiza. Although here and there could be seen a native structure of flat-roofed Mediterranean style, billboards and broken bits of recent civilization were much more prevalent. Several high-rise apartments and hotels were under construction, utilizing the familiar construction cranes which, Charles once told Susan, "roost on the skyline of every big city on earth."

Charles pointed out the taxi window. "This is San Jorge," he said. "My God, when I was here before all you could see were old women in black skirts that touched the ground or men driving donkeys." He sighed. "And the

They Are Ruining Ibiza

windmills . . . the ones around the airport are the only ones we've seen and they are obviously a tourist bureau plant. What happened to all the windmills?"

"I imagine the electric motor has taken over," Susan said.

"Not on Ibiza. Electricity's too uncertain. You take for granted you'll have a brown-out, or an orange-out, at least once a night."

✤✤✤✤

Charles tapped the driver on the shoulder. "*Señor . . . momentito, por favor. Alto.*"

The driver stopped the cab and looked back at him. "*Que?*"

"The bridge . . . *Aquí.*"

The driver smiled and nodded. "*Sí, el puente romano.*"

Charles looked down at an ancient stone structure which crossed a dry bed. "This bridge was built by the Romans," he told Susan. "It's the oldest public structure still in use on Ibiza . . . but, my God, the river's gone." He turned to the driver, "*Donde está el rio?*"

The driver gestured. "El rio ees dry; las turistas drink the agua." He grinned and pointed down to the dry riverbed.

"But this is the only river in the Balearics . . . *el rio solamente de los Baleares, no es verdad?*"

The driver smiled again, "*Sí, pero ya no rio.*"

Charles looked hurt. "'Now there is no river?' But this is the most famous spot on Ibiza. Everything through the centuries mentions this bridge or shows it in engravings . . . with the river flowing under it."

Susan shrugged, "But not now; they've got tourists instead of a river."

"*Sí*," the driver smiled at Susan, "*hay turistas en lugar del rio.*"

Three

Charles awoke feeling tired and still sleepy. He had forgotten to set his wristwatch for local time and had no idea how early it might be. Susan stirred in the other single bed, turning to him.

"What time is it?"

A. C. Greene

"I can only guess. I'd say it's 5 A.M., from the way I feel. This goddamn sorry bed . . . and don't say it's my age, like you did last night."

"I apologize for last night, darling. But you made such a scene when we checked in."

"My God . . . of course I made a scene. I wanted a double bed and that numbskull at the desk simply would not accommodate me. I knew what kind of a night we faced in these godawful painful cots. How many overweight Germans do you suppose it took to mash these springs flat? This hotel is a tourist trap of the worst sort."

"I think it's all rather nice. The people staying here seem happy enough with things—and the Ibiza electrical service was excellent. Not a brownout I could catch."

"Don't try to be cute. Give it time; there'll be brownouts on Ibiza."

"Oh, Charles, you're just cross because you have jet lag. And I know it's not 5 A.M. What does your watch say?"

"I forgot to reset the damn thing. It's still on American time. Besides, Spain is on the twenty-four-hour clock."

"You said you used twenty-four-hour time in the Navy. You told me to just subtract twelve from whatever the number is."

"And how is that going to help me if it's 5 A.M.? Subtract twelve and get minus seven o'clock?" he rolled up on one elbow. "I've forgotten most of what I learned in the U.S. Navy. Remember, I was in the Navy before you

They Are Ruining Ibiza

were born, you charming little thirty-six . . . and since I've mentioned the magic number, with all its provocative associations, why don't you come over here and get in bed with me?" He patted the sheet beside him.

She smiled, "Oh, no. I'm going out and stroll the beach."

"Are you going right now?"

"Certainly I am. Don't look so pathetic. Get up and come with me. I want to see Ibiza while I have the chance."

He frowned. "It's too early to get up."

"Well, you sleep another hour. I'm going to go dip a toe in the Mediterranean. I've never touched those fabled waters."

He pulled the sheet over his face. "Two-to-one you think you are going topless."

"I may; especially if you stay in bed."

He laughed, still beneath the sheet. "You'll freeze your pretties."

❈❈❈❈

After Susan left the room he discovered he could not go back to sleep. Damn it, it disturbed him that she was so determined to go topless. Not the morality of it—after all, what could be more moral than a woman's breasts that a baby wanted to suck? It disturbed a topic he couldn't talk to her about: age. Damn age to hell. She'd never bring it up, but why would she want to parade around topless except to see how many younger men she could catch leering at her? It would be different if she hung down to the waist, but that thirty-six she was so proud of . . . it was delightful.

But just now, refusing to get in his bed—was she laughing off lovemaking more and more often, or was it his imagination? It seemed to him it was happening too frequently of late. She pretended she was understanding, that she recognized he was not always as alert (she called it) as a young man—but damn the idea. If he were nearer her age, damn if he'd have let her leave the hotel room. Damn if she'd have wanted to leave. That was the bitter truth. If he were nearer her age she would have come crawling over to his bed, invited or not.

"Screw it," he said aloud, addressing himself. He'd promised not to let himself think this kind of thing when he married Susan. This doubt about age. He'd had enough doubt with Harriet; wondering, those last months . . . those last years, not about age, but about love, and (he hated to say it), about admiration.

And where was Harriet now? Jesus, wouldn't it be something if they both wound up visiting Led at the same time? He didn't want to see Harriet, if he could help it. She was a defeat. Married to her for twenty-two years, and then the whole thing was over in a puff . . . one day; not even thinking about it when he had waked up that morn-

They Are Ruining Ibiza

ing, it was over by night. Harriet made him feel like a failure. Was he getting the same way with Susan?

Suddenly a terrible racket began outside the room, a deep growling which he recognized as an engine, and an intermittent clash and clang, then a tremendous splash and thud. What in hell was going on? He pulled back the floor-length curtains and saw what the noise was about. A jetty was being built along the bay side of the hotel. As he watched, huge trucks delivered mammoth rocks to a crane, and each time the crane dropped one of the boulders into the bay.

"No rest for the wicked," he muttered to himself, then wondered, as he always did, if the quotation was "wicked" or "weary." "I fit both categories," he told himself, "wicked and weary . . . They're ruining Ibiza," he muttered, watching another huge vehicle with another mammoth rock come roaring up the dirt road along the jetty out to the crane.

Surveying the bay for the first time in daylight, his eyes felt as if a strobe light had flashed directly into them. There, anchored in the bay, a yacht was flying the bold red, white and blue and single star of the Texas state flag.

What's that son of a bitch doing here? Look at that! Some goddamn rich oil man. Jesus! I come all the way to Ibiza and what's the first thing I see when I look out my hotel window? A goddamn boat flying the Texas flag! Talk about provincial. What the hell's somebody from Texas doing here in the first place? The travel agent told him there were not very many Americans on the island . . . and now, a goddamn Texan.

He turned from the wide window and tore into his kit, extracting his shaving gear and his blow dryer. He took them to the bathroom and flipped the electrical switch on and off several times. "Hell's bells!" he exclaimed, disappointed that the electrical system worked.

❋❋❋❋

The sunbathers were out in force when Charles and Susan left their room, even though the day had not heated up very much. The English-speaking man at the desk told them that only certain beaches on Ibiza were *playas naturas* but that by now no one remembered or cared. "The turistas are *desnudo* wherever they decide."

"I hope you didn't actually do your topless act during your beach walk," Charles said to Susan after they left the hotel.

"Except for two little boys who were trying to fish, I was alone, and it's no fun if no one's looking," she said.

"I knew that's the way you'd feel," he said back to her.

Susan laughed, "Oh, Charles, you are so predictable. I wouldn't dream of going topless except with you. With your permission, master."

"Nonsense. You've got it backward. You'd be out there if it *weren't* for me."

They Are Ruining Ibiza

At the hotel beach they walked along the high embankment and looked down on the sunbathers reclining on the canvas loungers which were rented from the beach boys. One woman, lying on her back, was nude; ironically, her quite visible pubic area was carefully shaved so that a string suit would not reveal too much. As he was observing the woman, Susan grabbed his arm, whispering feverishly, "Look! That *man's* nude. I can see his . . . penis!"

"Sauce for the goose, goose," Charles chuckled and patted her briskly on her bottom. "Now, do you still want to come down here and parade your pussy?" He regarded the nude man scornfully, "Someone should inform Mr. Macho that what's on display is in no way outstanding." He shrugged, "There is only one thing uglier than a man's member, and that's a woman's . . . "

"Hush, Charles, I know what you are about to say and I've heard it before. And I wasn't going to 'parade my pussy' as you put it. I merely wanted to go topless."

"But regardless of what you say, you *are* willing to lie out there and display 'it,' aren't you?"

She smiled, "Some men seem to think such things are attractive, even if you don't."

Charles hugged her, "You win, and if you ever run off of a morning again while I'm begging you to get into the sack with me, I'll trade you in on one of these European imports."

A group of young, just budding girls, cautiously, with much giggling, lowered their bikini tops for a few moments, then hugged themselves as some boys their age came into view. Trucks roared along the causeway with ton after ton of rocks, the drivers slowing to see the topless females at the hotel beach.

Charles and Susan got into the taxi the hotel had called for them. Charles asked the fare to San Lorenzo and the driver took out the fare card and pointed to the number. The cabs on Ibiza did not have meters.

The ride north from Santa Eulalia took them quickly out of the town and through a series of crossroads to the *Es Moli* gallery where, Led said several letters ago, he had shown some of his work. *Es Moli* gallery was situated by itself on a road which appeared to Charles to lead nowhere. There was a sign on the gallery's front door which notified the public that it opened at 1700 hours.

"Good heavens . . . is there anywhere around here we can wait?" Susan asked.

"Wait, hell. That's nearly seven hours to wait. I won't do it here."

Charles addressed the driver, "*Dónde es el estanco San Lorenzo?*"

The driver smiled broadly and said, "*Ah, . . estanco San Lorenzo es tres kilometros.*"

"*Cuanto mas?*" Charles asked.

The driver shrugged, "*Quién sabe? Poquito mas.*"

"He thinks you're broke, the way you pester him about the fare," Susan said.

They Are Ruining Ibiza

"Well, as I've had to tell you so often, my trusting one, we are tourists, and there's nowhere on the globe I know of that tourists aren't considered fair game. It's obligatory. To screw the tourist is part of the international code of honor."

"Oh, dear . . . when will I learn not to get the Reverend Dr. Martyn started on one of his sermons?"

The drive to the *estanco* was short, and by now the taxi driver seemed to understand what Charles and Susan were doing. Charles was somewhat surprised to find the *estanco* really did resemble an American 7-Eleven store. The manager, who was also the postal clerk, was talking with the driver and Charles could hear the words "*americano*" and "*hijo*" (son) being used several times. He decided to add a detail.

He stroked his chin as he described Led's red beard (*"barba roja"*), and the other men began doing the same thing, muttering, *"barba roja"* and nodding their heads. Despite this being one of the places where Led had said he picked up mail, the storekeeper seemed only vaguely aware of *un americano* with *barba roja*. He and the taxi driver decided the place to ask for Led was more properly up the *carretera* a few kilometers at a bar and eating place called "*Es Pins.*" This time Charles did not ask the driver how much it would be but the driver seemed pleased to announce, "*Ya no hay,*" which Charles interpreted as "It's no additional."

A. C. Greene

The drive to *Es Pins* was short. A dog began to bark as Charles and the driver approached what Charles took to be the restaurant. A tall, older man came out to them, shouting a greeting, and the driver addressed him as Don José. The large dog with Don José persisted in nosing Charles in the seat of his trousers no matter how much Charles tried to push the dog's head away. An old woman, dressed entirely in Ibicenco black, shouted a command, "*perro!*" and the beast trotted over to her and sat on its haunches. The old Ibicenco asked pleasantly, "*Su hijo?*"

Charles answered, "*Sí.*"

The old man asked again, "*Tiene una barba roja, verdad?*"

Charles agreed. The man pointed up the road and instructed the driver "*Da Vd. la derecha cerca de las bombas de petroleo.*" The driver exchanged a few more words with the old couple and they departed amidst a shower of repeated *"Adios."*

Back in the cab, Susan asked, "What was your attraction for the dog? He looked like he wanted to make love to you."

"He's almost big enough," Charles told her. "There's your genuine Ibiza, right there," he pointed to the elderly couple. "Don José and María. They dress, talk, and think *Eivissenc*. Their place here is famous. They prove that sanity can be retained, even in this modern world."

"Did he know Led?"

They Are Ruining Ibiza

"Indeed he did. We are headed, if my Spanish is sufficient, for the petrol pumps where we shall take a right turn and find Led."

But turning at the gasoline pumps only succeeded in taking the taxi down an increasingly rougher road. As they forded a tiny trickle of water, two pretty young girls approached on bicycles and when asked, the older girl informed them no one lived on the road but *un scultor alemán con una esposa mas grande*.

"What did she say?" Susan asked.

Charles smiled, "She said, as near as I can translate, that no one lives down this road but a German sculptor with '*una esposa grande*'—a great big wife."

As they returned to the petrol pumps and the main road, Susan said to Charles, "I think we have been done in by politeness. You know? The Spanish simply do not like to disappoint you by saying they don't know. They have to tell you what they think you want to hear, even if it's a guess."

Charles decided they should return to the gallery and try to arouse the owner, whose name he had somewhere in his wallet. When they arrived at *Es Moli* the second time, Charles walked to the rear of the building and called out, "*Stefano . . . Señor Stefano?*"

A tall, blonde-haired woman appeared and said to him, "Steven isn't here." She was English. Susan had joined Charles and they asked about Led and his whereabouts, explaining that their cablegrams had apparently gone astray.

"Not unusual for Ibiza," the woman said.

Susan asked, "Could he be living in some little town around here? Santa Gertrudis, maybe? He wrote that it was one of his favorite places."

The English woman shrugged. "I'm so sorry," she said, "but I simply do not know where Ledyard lives. I see the girl, his wife . . . what's her name, Trixie? . . . once in a while in Sant'ulalie, but not up here at the gallery."

Charles took the envelope out of his pocket and showed her. "This is where he is supposed to get his mail. The *estanco* San Lorenzo. But the man there seems not to recall ever seeing Led. We've looked over most of this section, I believe."

The blonde woman nodded, throwing her long hair back with her head. "Yes . . . well, I would suggest, if I may, that you go to Sandy's Bar in Sant'ulalie. The arty folk collect there in the afternoons. It's an English bar. Not native, you understand. Sooner or later everyone on Ibiza who speaks English goes there. I'm sure you may either find your son there or someone will know where he is. I simply can't help you." She blew quite a lot of smoke toward the ceiling and shook her hair again.

Charles and Susan returned to the road where the taxi waited. "Well, what do you think?" Charles asked.

"What else is there? The old Ibicencos at *Es Pin* don't know him, that's apparent; the *estanco* owner either doesn't

They Are Ruining Ibiza

know or thinks you're the *Guardia Civil*. That leaves Sandy's Bar, doesn't it?"

In the taxi Charles said to the driver, "*Donde es Sandy's Bar?*" The driver smiled, "*Sí, por el caballo.*" The little Fiat spun around quickly on the gravel and they headed back to Santa Eulalia. As they drove along the narrow road, Charles whispered to Susan, "I wonder what he meant saying it was 'by the horse'?"

"Is that what he said?" Susan asked. "Maybe he meant you."

The highway, as they neared Santa Eulalia, was jammed with honking, roaring automobiles, trucks, and mopeds. "I have not seen one American car," Charles said. "Imagine what it would be like trying to get a Cadillac or a Lincoln through this mess."

At the *Plaza d'España*, the taxi driver turned left and took them to the second street, where he stopped and pointed triumphantly, "*El caballo!*" They then saw what he meant; the sign which proclaimed "Sandy's Bar" pictured a stylized running horse.

Sandy's Bar was a small, low-ceilinged room, with track lights that spotlighted various tables and seats rather than furnishing room illumination. The bar itself was well lighted, but was not much bigger than a corner in someone's den, and the tall stools around it, cane with leather seats, looked handmade, as did the other pieces of furniture. Several leather cushioned chairs and two sofas sat along the walls, and an open fireplace still had the past winter's ashes in it. The place gave off a homey air yet was quite Spanish. When they walked in a man was hanging a large painting on the left-hand wall. Backing across the narrow room to gauge its placement, he brushed Susan's left foot.

"Oh, very sorry," the man said, "damned clumsy of me." He had a soft English accent.

Susan grimaced and reached down to rub a toe. "I had my foot in the wrong place; thank God you're wearing jogging shoes," she said, then looking at the picture, asked, "Is that yours?"

"Well, yes, I painted it. I'm hoping in a few days it *won't* be mine. It's for sale."

The large painting depicted a group of elongated figures engaged in what appeared to be a beach picnic. Most of the women in the painting were bare breasted and two of the male figures were bearded.

"It's very nice . . . is it Ibiza?" she asked.

"The bloke with th' pirate's beard . . . that virile chap . . . that's me," the bartender said. The artist laughed, "Topless goes, but I leave Jon's virility to the imagination."

The bartender spoke to them, "You're Americans, aren't you? Welcome to Sandy's Bar."

"Are you Sandy?" Charles asked.

"I'm Jonathan," the bartender said.

"He owns the place now," the painter said. "Sandy sold out and retired. Too much success."

They Are Ruining Ibiza

"I'm attempting to avoid that fate by letting artists like Michael hang his trashy canvases in here," Jonathan said.

"Did you paint the horse?" Susan asked the painter, who looked puzzled. "The horse?"

"The sign, you twit," Jonathan said, nodding toward the front door. "Oh, *el caballo*," the painter laughed. "No, that came with the bar. Sandy took in the original on some painter's tab."

"I might find my son here, a woman at San Lorenzo told me," Charles said. "At *Es Moli* gallery . . . very long, blonde hair," he offered.

Jonathan and Michael looked at each other, "Would that be Phyllis or Barbara, I wonder?" the bartender asked.

"Not much help," Jonathan said. "Phyllis and Barbara both have very long, blonde hair and both can be prevailed upon to keep the gallery when Stefano's ashore."

"I imagine it was Phyllis," Michael said.

"Who is your son?" Jonathan asked.

"His name is Ledyard Martyn and his wife is . . ." Jonathan was nodding and before Charles could finish said, "Yes, of course . . . Led and Christy. So you're his parents?"

Susan smiled, "Well . . . I'm not his mother."

Jonathan smiled back, "To be sure; I'd venture you're a sister, then?"

"She's my wife," Charles said.

Jonathan quickly added, "You're a most fortunate fellow, Mr. Martyn."

A. C. Greene

Susan laughed, "Thank you."

Charles said, "I'm pleased to find someone on this island who knows Led. He was supposed to have met us when we arrived, but so far, we can't uncover a clue as to where he is."

"Afraid I can't say where he is. Actually, he hasn't been in here in some time; last winter, I expect," Jonathan said.

"Do you know his address?" Susan asked. Jonathan smiled, "No such thing on Ibiza, dear, except in town. A few of the *fincas* have names."

"*C'an Lluqui* . . . if I'm pronouncing it right, that's the name of the place he's renting," Charles said.

"No help, either," Jonathan said. "Must be a dozen *C'an Lluquis* on Ibiza; like *Isidoro Macabich* street, one in every town," he winked at Susan. "Macabich was the great island intellectual, dear. Historian." He gestured, "Let the bar set up drinks for you . . . on the house while you wait for someone who knows the present whereabouts of young Ledyard Martyn."

"What about the patio? It looks inviting." Susan asked, "May we sit there?"

"Of course. Just push the old Duke out of the way if he's gone to sleep on the couch," Jonathan looked around the corner of the bar toward the rear patio. "No, the old fellow's working on his memoirs. You're safe."

Susan glanced out and saw a white-bearded man seated in a chair at one side of the patio. "Is he a real duke?"

Jonathan laughed, "Says he is. Don't say where."

They Are Ruining Ibiza

"From the Channel Islands," Michael contributed. Jonathan laughed again, "I'm from Jersey, Channel Islands, while our Michael's of the Isle of Wight."

Charles considered, "I've never had one of those native Ibicenco drinks . . . *Fragiola* or *hierbas*. Which would you recommend?"

Jonathan shook his head, "Oh, dear, neither, this early in the afternoon. Stick to the tried and true. Try a San Miguel. Good beer." Charles agreed and suggested Susan have a gin and tonic. When they had ordered, Jonathan nodded toward the patio. "Find a place, I'll deliver."

They seated themselves on a low wicker sofa in the rock-floored patio. One side was sheltered beneath an ancient fig tree, loaded with disregarded black figs and sharing space with grapevines and tall, green, spearlike plants growing from pots. Three low doors, with lintels sagging, were located along the right-hand wall. One apparently led to living quarters and the others were marked "*Damas*" and "*Hombres*." The rock and brick walls were whitewashed, and in the corner nearest the bar was a little whitewashed stucco structure with a small tile roof on it.

"That's the cistern, there in the corner," Charles told Susan. "All the older buildings have one. That used to be the way you obtained water on Ibiza, catch it off the roof during the rainy season. Now, I suppose, it's piped in from wells." He looked closely at the cistern, "How the mighty have fallen. It houses the stereo speakers."

Jonathan brought their drinks and then made a tilting gesture with his empty hand, "Cheers!"

Charles took a sip of beer and leaned toward Susan, speaking softly. "Does it seem to you that these people are protecting Led?"

Susan looked at him with a frown, "Protecting him, from what?"

"From us . . . from me."

"Oh, Charles, don't get paranoid. Just because our cables didn't reach him. Having observed the lifestyle, I'd say it is altogether possible for cables to go astray or lie in postal boxes for weeks without being disturbed."

"Nonsense; I don't care what they say. In the first place, I think the cables arrived."

"So, why does that mean they're protecting Led? It seems to me they'd be eager to see you find him, in case his painting's not paying off."

"Oh, I'm sure his mother supplies him with cash when he needs it."

"All right, Charles . . . they're protecting him. But let's enjoy this afternoon. This is a wonderful place to enjoy it and we're as likely to run into Led and Christy here as anywhere."

"I don't like the idea . . . either they're protecting him or he doesn't want us to find him, or both."

"As you so frequently say, Charles, 'nonsense.' There's no reason he should hide from you. Or me. Led and I have always gotten along very well, you know."

They Are Ruining Ibiza

"He's never forgiven me for what he thinks I did to Harriet . . . ditching his mother for this young chick."

Susan shook her head furiously, "Charles, that's past history. You and . . . his mother . . . that was concluded before you even met me. Led introduced us, if you recall. Besides, we're not exactly newlyweds . . . and as for you marrying 'this young chick,' we've both been married before."

Charles, drinking from the bottle, looked at the label and shook his head. "I've always thought San Miguel beer to be a Filipino beer. This says it is brewed and bottled here in Spain."

"Maybe it's like Coca Cola, bottled everywhere," Susan said.

Charles studied the label, then said, "Susan, do you ever think about Carl? Does his memory bother you?"

She shook her head. "There was nothing memorable about my marriage to Carl."

"But, didn't you make plans and have ambitions, that sort of thing?"

"Carl was a jerk. He had plans, but they were all his. Mine never counted. Stop thinking about Carl. I haven't seen him in eight years and there's no reason I ever need to see him again."

"Weren't you ever in love with him? Didn't you marry him for love?"

"Why this inquisition about somebody you never met? If I loved him it was over a long time before I met you."

A. C. Greene

"Was there anyone else, between times?"

"Between times? Between times of what? Are you implying I slept around? I don't know whether it makes you feel better or worse, but I was shockingly chaste, between husbands, if that's the 'between times' you refer to. I'm your wife, in fact and memory."

"How very poetic," Charles said. But he couldn't entirely stifle the question: Did she miss it, that constant sexual demanding a young wife got from a young husband? Susan had never mentioned what Carl was, or wasn't, like in bed. Perhaps that had been the best part, the part that had held the marriage together as long as it did. Sometimes he could not keep from seeing her making love with Carl, abandoned to pleasure, as she tended to be, even with him . . . oh, God; stop it!

❊❊❊❊

The bar's front door could be observed from where he was sitting on the patio and Charles could catch sight of Led or Christy should either appear. The crowd was increasing, many of them apparently regulars who looked on Sandy's as a second home, dropping packages or coats on empty chairs while they stood against the bar, waiting for a first round of drinks. The patio was filling with many nationalities, not all European. Charles, looking at them, thought: the young, the young . . . their terribly

They Are Ruining Ibiza

casual waste of time. Time, time, time—that commodity only experience puts a value on.

Susan took his hand and squeezed it, "Let's savor the moment, Charles. This is what I hoped Ibiza would be."

From the stereo speakers housed in their little cistern came a nasal English voice singing, *"Maybe I'm right, maybe I'm wrong, loving you, dear, as I do . . . ."*

"Listen," Charles said to Susan. "Do you recognize that song?"

She frowned slightly, listening, "No, I'm afraid I don't."

"It's from the thirties; It's called 'Guilty.' That must be an old recording." Charles sat listening, "Just think, that singer's older than I am, much older, but we're hearing him just as he was in 1931 or '32."

He asked Susan, "Did you know that I did my MA thesis on the songs and ballads of the thirties and forties? 'Popular Balladry as Creative Motive.' That's how I met Harriet. She was working in a record shop."

Charles hummed the tune coming from the speakers, then joined the singer, " . . . *if it's a crime, then I'm guilty, guilty of loving you.*" He stopped.

Susan nudged him, "Keep singing. You're charming." Charles shook his head, sadly, "I don't remember all the lyrics, just a few phrases." The voice on the tape continued: ". . . *you go your way and I will go mine, but I'll feel for you just the same . . . .*"

Without a word he got to his feet.

A. C. Greene

"Charles . . . where are you going?"

He looked at her, and it appeared his eyes were about to fill with tears. His mouth was open, as if he were trying to remember what he wanted to say. In that isolated instant a woman's voice from somewhere on the patio suddenly stated, "Everyone in Ibiza is getting rich," and a male voice replied, "The Senator is rich already."

"Then why is he building the jetty?"

"So he can get richer."

Charles, still standing, asked hoarsely, "Another beer?"

"This is a gin and tonic, dear."

"Another, then? I'll get them."

"Yes, this actually has gin in it."

The elderly Duke was now working the *Guardian* crossword with a fountain pen and muttering to himself, flinging ink to the stone floor occasionally to clear his pen. Another couple, dark and exotic, passed where Susan sat, the woman's full skirt brushing against Susan. "*Pardonnez moi,*" the woman said huskily.

Susan smiled, "*Bien entendu!*" The smell of musky perfume was quite strong. Two hundred an ounce, Susan thought.

Charles brought the drinks, putting her gin and tonic on the small table in front of her. He lifted the brown beer bottle to his lips, then paused. "I know what it is," he said.

"What what is?"

They Are Ruining Ibiza

"Why they're protecting Led. It's Harriet. She's here on Ibiza. With Led."

"Charles, you haven't the slightest notion Harriet is here . . . and you haven't any reason to think people are protecting Led. He and Christy are probably camping on some beach. We haven't looked everywhere."

"Everyone we've come into contact with knows him. His mother's with him and he's told them to keep us away."

Susan sighed, "My God, are you going to ruin this entire trip just because Led didn't meet us at the airport?"

"It's more than that. Can't you feel it? There's a funny kind of tense casualness in everybody when I mention Led being my son."

"Are you including the taxi driver? He went much farther trying to help than a New York cabbie would have gone."

"Oh, come on, Susan. You know what I mean. Something definitely isn't adding up. Ibiza isn't that big. Somebody is bound to know where Led is and why he doesn't want us to find him."

A thin voice, barely distinguishable as a man's, complained, "The gypsies have ruined *Es Penya*," and a deeper voice, barely distinguishable as a woman's, declared, "It's not gypsies, Lawrence darling . . . it's hippies, American hippies." Another woman, in brusque, impatient tones, snorted, "For God's sake, Clara, hippies went out with tie-

A. C. Greene

dye denims. If there are any left they're older than you are. What's ruined *Es Penya* is druggies; European druggies."

Michael, the artist, came through the doorway from the bar and nodded to Charles and Susan. "Come join us," Susan called.

"May I?" he asked, dropping onto the sofa beside her. He had a beer in one hand. "I wanted to tell you in privacy . . . didn't want Jon to hear. Led's been staying away from Sandy's. Somewhat of a tab, for one thing."

"I can take care of that," Charles said.

"Oh, no, no . . . it's also rather personal, I believe. Some mischief Jon exiled Led for. Not welcome for a few months. Happens all the time to us regulars. Jon's a real tyrant."

"But he seemed so friendly," Susan said.

"Oh, he's a fine enough person. If you'd come in with Led, I daresay there'd have been only sunshine and smiles. But I wanted to explain why you're not apt to find Led here. Also, to tell you, Led's *finca* is rather hard to locate. Most difficult to get to unless one has a guide. It's very off the highway."

"Tell us how to get there and we'll hire a taxi," Charles said.

"I'm afraid that's the problem," Michael said. "You see, a taxi simply will not take you there, the roads are in such shape. Go as far as the water company, perhaps, but no farther."

"The water company?" Susan asked.

They Are Ruining Ibiza

"Morna Spring where they bottle water. It's about halfway to Led's house from the *camino*, but the road rather peters out beyond, and it's a bit far to leg it."

"Do you have his telephone number, or does he have one?"

"Good lord, no. Telephones are a great luxury on Ibiza. Out in the country mere installation can cost ten thousand American. Not even great restaurants like Ama Lur have a telephone."

"What about Led's automobile? He told us he'd swapped a painting for some sort of German car, *el vehiculo rojo* he called it. How does it make it, if the road's so terrible?"

"Oh, yes . . . the Red Baron," the artist laughed. "If you could see it you would understand. It's not exactly a new model. In addition, I believe Christy took the Red Baron when she left."

Charles and Susan looked at each other. "When she left? Left for where?" Charles asked.

Michael hesitated. "I'm sorry . . . I supposed you knew. They've split. Christy and Led. Some time back; three or four months. She went to Formentera, took the Red Baron with her. Living with an Italian fellow, I understand. Musician. Name's Baletti."

Charles said softly, "Jesus . . . why didn't somebody tell me?" He looked at Susan, "Why didn't Led tell us?"

Michael said, "Perhaps I should have waited and let Led tell you, but I supposed you knew."

51

A. C. Greene

Charles shook off the painter's apology, "No, no . . . that's fine, you telling us. It explains a lot."

Michael, still contrite, said, "May I offer to take you to Led's farm house, then? If you can wait until tomorrow morning. If he's not at the *finca*, we can go up to Cala Boix, then maybe *el mercado* at Es Cana. Led shows paintings there sometimes."

"What's *el mercado*?" Susan asked.

"Just a big outdoor market, mostly European crafts people. A few Americans. I drop off a canvas from time to time."

"Where's this place Led lives?" Charles asked.

"In the Morna Valley. Back from the shore a few kilometers you have a lovely hill country. Old *fincas* and those ancient terraces that date back to the Romans. It's quite Mediterranean, once one gets off the *carretera*. You should go up to the northern end to see the real Ibiza: Cala Xarraca, San Miguel, Santa Gertrudis . . . that's the pure Ibiza; the fellows in their red nightcaps and white breeches dancing with the young women in their preg clothes, weird Ibicenco music . . . all drums, wood flutes and tambourines. Catch 'em on a feast day and you're right back in the sixteenth century."

"And the rest of the time they drive a taxi?" Susan laughed.

Charles said to Michael, "Have you lived here long?"

"Ten years, more or less. An unfortunate marriage somewhere in there."

They Are Ruining Ibiza

"Ledyard's been here three. He's wanted to come back to Ibiza since he was here as a boy with his mother and me."

Michael stood up, "I've some business to do hereabouts, so shall we meet in the plaza, tomorrow . . . tenish? You can visit city hall or make friends with the *Guardia Civil*. They're headquartered on the plaza, too."

After Michael left them, Charles said to Susan, "Well, at least we know why everyone's been protecting Led. Because of this thing with Christy."

"But if Michael were protecting Led, why offer to take us to Led's house? I think we've been victims of unplanned coincidence, starting with our cables going astray."

"No, it's part of the game; you wait . . . Led won't be there."

Susan shook her head, "So if he's not, it's the coincidence thing again. Darling, stop being so spooky. Life's mostly coincidences."

"I'll stop being spooky when there's nothing to be spooky about . . . when those 'unplanned coincidences' of yours become little 'accidents' that enhance the pleasure of our visit. But no, you say, none of this is planned. It's all accidental, a mass of unrelated disturbances which just dropped from the sky, like we did when we decided to come to this blasted island. Coincidence? Don't believe a word of it!"

Susan smiled. "My God, King Canute himself couldn't overcome that tide of rhetoric. Forgive me for ever bringing up the possibility."

Four

He had been introduced to Susan in Washington, D.C. by Led, who was working in Joe Roderick's office helping that self-appointed ex-Stanford ass arrange cultural exchange programs and swap American flautists for Polish pianists, or make sure Danish ballet troupes played places like Salt Lake City and Omaha and didn't spend their entire visit in New York or San Francisco.

Led had persuaded him to attend one of the seemingly every-night gatherings of which Washington appointees partook. Charles had scrupulously avoided any such the

They Are Ruining Ibiza

three weeks he had been in town working with PBS and the Library of Congress on the "Writers of the American Dream" series that was dropped when both Bill Moyers and James Earl Jones were found to be unavailable.

Led introduced him to Susan Roman, explaining she was connected to some Oversight Committee in the capitol. Perhaps it was just the age difference, but Led seemed slightly afraid of her, as though he'd just as soon get her into the hands of someone more competent at the party game than he was. Charles decided she must not control the purse strings of any cultural activity, otherwise Roderick would have been squiring her himself, because she was certainly the best-looking female in the room.

Led told his father, when he introduced her, that Susan Roman was familiar with his work, "and she's a keen lady," he added, which introduction irked Charles, since ladies, keen or unkeen, didn't need this twenty-two-year-old male to apprise him of their keenness.

Susan, after Led had made his escape, told Charles, "I've always wanted to meet the author of *Anabella*."

Charles smiled frigidly and said, "I haven't written a book titled *Anabella*." Susan blushed and exclaimed, "God, what a faux pas; you're Charles Martyn, not Marty Martin the novelist. Are you any kin?"

"I believe we spell our names differently," Charles answered, and might have been more than a bit annoyed if he hadn't found her so attractive.

A. C. Greene

"Dr. Charles Martyn . . . of course. *The Last Word on the American Novel*; we used it at Mills College."

"*A Last Look at*, not *The Last Word on*," he corrected her.

"Dr. Martyn, I never thought I would see the day when I would actually meet you." He could tell she was putting him on; at least, he felt sure she was.

Charles resurrected his frigid smile and said, "I didn't realize I was so old that people your age lost all hope of glimpsing me alive . . . which is what I suppose you meant?"

Actually, the evening had gone smoothly and he fell in love with her quite early, even after she had announced proudly that her mother, an anthropologist, had four inches in *Who's Who*. "Oh, God, I've done it again," she caught herself. "I suppose you're going to tell me you have ten?"

"More like five. I eliminated all my out-of-print book titles and honorary degrees."

"You were a perfect jerk," she told him later, quickly adding, "And don't say, 'Nobody's perfect.'"

She told him she was divorced, had no children, and had reclaimed her maiden name after her marriage was over. At first he felt awkward with her because she was so much younger than he was, taking her to a few cultural and artistic gatherings there in Washington. Then he grew proud of her in a way he'd never been with Harriet, even when young. He and Susan both agreed they were not interested in each other's pasts, married or unmarried. He told her he was disgusted and disillusioned with the academic world and she told him, "I don't bruise easily." Then they laughed and told each other they neither one meant it.

When he returned to New York, after the PBS series collapsed, he tried to bring himself to ask her to come up and spend a weekend with him, the way any young stud under age forty would, but he was strangely reticent, old-fashioned, afraid to try to go to bed with her. It was months before they did. The first time they made love, he cried. Martyn cracked . . . but he couldn't think of himself as "Martyn" in that moment; he became the other man, the persistent figure that stays just beyond reality, that represents (without being acknowledged) the ideal at one point, the actual at another. His tears were from joy, discovery, freedom: and he was both apprentice and sorcerer. It was something he had never experienced before, and he refused to say a word, as he held her, unwilling to turn the moment loose, because it could not be preserved and perhaps could never be repeated. One morning, still in bed, he said to Susan, "Let's quit playing games and get married." And, surprisingly, she easily agreed.

❈❈❈❈

A. C. Greene

"Are you going to wear a skirt?" Charles asked, frowning, as they prepared to meet Michael.

Susan looked down, then said, "Certainly. I bought this skirt just for the trip to Ibiza."

"But why wear a skirt? Why not wear jeans? Getting in and out of a car, a skirt can be awkward . . . especially one that short."

"Charles, what are you trying to say . . . that you want me not to expose myself, not show my legs? Do you think Michael might make a pass at me?"

"I wouldn't say yes or no to that question; and my initial inquiry was more from curiosity than censure."

"I find it hard to tell the difference. You seldom approve of things you're curious about. And remember, if you will, we went through all this when we got married. I told you then, our age difference didn't count. But I'm not going to dress like your granny. Do you think, after thirty-six years, I can't manage a skirt? Or that I'm going to go around showing my underpants because I choose to wear a skirt? You're jealous. You think I'm trying to attract men, don't you?"

"You can't help it."

"No, I can't, and you should accept that."

"Of course I accept it, otherwise I might be fighting a duel every week, my dear. I'm proud to have a wife toward whom other men can't help but turn their lust and their attention. Very proud." Charles was obviously wanting to appease her.

They Are Ruining Ibiza

"Well, I can't do anything about men's lust or their attention either. If, as you tell me, these Ibicenco men can lust after women draped in black from head to foot," Susan moved her hands downward across her body, "as they have done for centuries, then we must conclude there's something in the male that reacts regardless of what a woman is wearing."

"Or, *not* wearing, as on modern Ibiza."

"Besides, we're five thousand miles from anybody who knows us. I want to have a little freedom; I want to try some of the things that all my life I've been told I mustn't try. I don't know how much longer I can go topless or wear a short skirt, or have a man give a damn whether or not I'm exposing myself. I'm not going to hop in bed with him just because some young stud sees me topless on the beach."

Charles smiled. "*Au contraire*, you'll have men watching any time you so much as cross your ankles in that garment. God forbid some over-passionate Mediterranean spies you reclining *au naturel* on the sand, or sees you scissoring to the crossroads when removing from an automobile."

Susan couldn't keep from grinning. "God, what a masculine metaphor. I'm surely not going to hop in bed with just any young stud who is overcome at seeing me 'scissor.'"

"I don't know; you might like it."

A. C. Greene

She patted his face. "I don't need any young studs, darling . . . all I want is once, just *once*, to do whatever I wish to do; experience the kind of freedom a man takes for granted all his life and a woman begins giving up the first time she puts on a bra."

❈❈❈❈

Charles and Susan left the hotel and walked toward the center of Santa Eulalia along the bay road which passed several other hotels and a tennis club. Once Charles halted his wife and went to a vacant site that had recently been bulldozed. He picked up a piece of broken tile. It was thick and primitive looking but the remaining portion of its glazed face showed artistic charm.

"This is old dirt, and obviously has been used over and over," he pronounced. "This tile was made a few hundred years back, maybe in Roman times, or Punic. I'm going to keep it."

Susan took the tile. "It's beautiful, isn't it? It looks Arabic."

"And certainly could be. The Moors were here, you know. Had a town called *Xarc*. If you dig enough I'll bet you can find Iberian Bronze Age culture."

"I'll take your word for it," Susan said, then picked up something. "Hey, here's a shard from the modern Vandal period," she handed him the neck of a blue plastic bottle. Charles looked at it distastefully. "We can thank our rich

They Are Ruining Ibiza

Texas friends for that cultural contribution," he said, pointing to the yacht with the Texas flag, moored out in the bay.

"You're not being fair, Dr. Martyn. That plastic bottle could have come from any boat that may have anchored here in the past twenty years."

"You can't convince me it's not from that oil man's yacht. The trouble with you, dear, is you don't know these people . . . these oil types. They have no regard for anything or anybody. They're spoiled, ruthless . . . and they're everywhere. They're the kind we saw in Maine last year; I wouldn't be surprised if it's not the same boat."

"Oh, Charles, be reasonable. Those yahoos in Maine were from New York and you know it. They were flying some New York yacht club pennant. You said you recognized one of the men. Knew him at school. And be fair to the Texans; you know nothing about them. You don't even know they're from Texas; anybody can fly a Texas flag. We have one ourselves . . . remember? Greg gave it to us."

"I'm not really talking about Texas or oil people. They're just symbolic. What I despise are the heedless bastards who find every little corner of paradise and muck it up, cheapen it. So goddamn insensitive they can't be hurt." He glared across the water at the boat. "Come on. I apologize for my tirade."

The plaza was shaded by old palm trees and a small fountain splashed timidly in their shade. A weathered monument paid homage to (Charles read aloud), "The

A. C. Greene

noble sons of Santa Eulalia for their humanitarian conduct during the sinking" (I think that's it) "of the *barco* 'Mallorca' in 1913." He nodded, "Don't you love the stateliness of the Spanish mind? Can you imagine how that inscription would read in bureaucratic federalese: 'Award designated for the citizens of the municipality of Santa E-u-ll-a-l-i-a'—they always make at least one mistake—'who rescued significant numbers of passengers, of all races and creeds, from the allegedly sinking ship *Mallorca* (Erected under Senate bill 441, the Heros/Heroines Act).'"

Susan laughed, "You would have made a wonderful bureaucrat."

When they were seating themselves on a concrete bench, slightly above the traffic of the highway, a tall, blond man burst out of the *Café Cosmi*, across the street, with a smaller man, apparently a waiter, choking him and bellowing something in protest. The blonde man finally thrust the other man from him, stood in the street for a moment yelling back at his assailant, then went purposefully to the whitewashed *ayuntamiento* where Charles and Susan could see him talking to a municipal policeman.

"He won't get to first base," Charles said. "He's complaining about a native and nothing will come of it."

As Charles spoke, the young blond man, still protesting, walked away. "He looks like an American," Susan said.

"That's not an American," Charles said. "An American would have knocked the shit out of that waiter."

They Are Ruining Ibiza

"Charles, what's come over you? And what about the stateliness of the Spanish mind?"

Michael, at the wheel of a small, battered auto, pulled to one side of the plaza and waved at them to join him. Getting in beside the driver, Charles said, "Stop at some petrol pump and I'll fill your tank."

Michael smiled, "Petrol pumps take a bit of finding. But my little French ma'moiselle here gets such amazing mileage we needn't worry."

Going out of Santa Eulalia, the countryside became an arrangement of low walls and plowed fields. Michael pointed to some extensive brick ruins and told them, "That's what remains of the island's sugar industry."

They turned off the *carretera*, or highway, onto a narrow asphalt *camino* which twisted among ancient olive trees and now and then an orchard. "Carobs," Michael said. "I suppose the carob groves are the last form of agriculture still practiced to any extent on Ibiza."

Susan asked, "What about the figs and grapes . . . everywhere I look I see clusters going to seed, or whatever figs and grapes do. Doesn't anybody pick them?"

"Not much," Michael told her. "It's so much easier to make your living off the *turistas*. I read in *Diario de Ibiza* that sixty-some-odd per cent of the island economy is now tourism. Even the salterns don't bring in half what they did. Why fuss with olives and figs or pick grapes? Spanish wine's cheaper, and they say olive oil's a headache to market."

A. C. Greene

Charles sighed, "Michael, they're ruining Ibiza. It may be easier to make a living . . . but *La Isla Blanca* that I knew is completely lost."

"Oh, I agree," Michael said, "but one does sympathize with the Ibicencos, they struggled to survive for centuries . . . and one does appreciate the paved roads now, although they're scarcely wide enough for the tour buses to pass."

"What is *La Isla Blanca*?" Susan asked.

"The White Isle," Charles told Susan. "That's the name some Spanish painter bestowed on Ibiza, I would guess, because of all the houses and churches shining white."

"I believe it comes from the almond tree blossoms each spring," Michael said, "but I must say, the white architecture has held up well; whitewashed and looking Moroccan; the marvelous old church fortresses atop their hills, protecting the inhabitants. To me they're more spiritual than the grand structures of España . . . even the Barcelona Gaudi doesn't do to me what *d'es Puig de Missa* church in Sant'ulalie does. You know, they really had to believe their religion back when these churches were built and every heathen pirate in Europe and Asia had a go at Ibiza. Something had to matter to them." He turned around and smiled, "Sorry to go on. I love the place. It sounds arty, but art's the way I make my living."

"You remind me of Led," Charles said. "You ever work with him?"

They Are Ruining Ibiza

"We painted together for a while last winter when I ran out of propane. It can get quite chilly, especially along this eastern side."

"What's Led painting? He hasn't sent us any photographs lately."

Michael smiled. "I call them vulvas . . . his paintings."

"Oh, dear," Susan said. "Are they done from life?"

"Oh, yes . . . well, actually, they're shells and flowers. You're familiar with some of the Georgia O'Keeffe paintings, aren't you? Her flowers and her clam shells? That's the sort of thing. Led has a whole series he calls 'Revelations.' Quite nice, really. Best things he's done, by my way of thinking."

The roadway was no longer paved; it twisted between the rock walls and bounced the car unmercifully. As they proceeded along a ridge, Michael made a sweeping gesture, "This is the Morna Valley, and I imagine some of these terraces were put down by our Punic predecessors. Every square meter of Ibiza was once terraced. Needed every cup of dirt that could be controlled. No matter how far up the island you go, the terraces climb with you. A good many are no bigger than a bed. The stones have to be redone every hundred years or so, but nobody really knows who put 'em in place first."

Charles asked why so many of the terraces looked neglected.

"It doesn't matter anymore. The terraces aren't used anyway. Ibiza doesn't need terraces, like it doesn't need windmills," Michael said.

Presently the road passed near a low, tin shed, "The water company," Michael announced. "Here's where a taxi would drop you off and refuse to go farther."

"I couldn't blame him," Susan said. "I'm not sure anything can survive this road."

Michael smiled, "The ma'moiselle has been doing this for a dozen years."

The rutted road ran at right angles to the fields, channeled between the rock walls and terraces. Twice they passed neat, whitewashed *fincas*, seeming to drive through the barnyards, but no animals were observed. "It's no longer a farm," Michael explained. "The owners of most of these places are Germans or Scandinavians. Led's *finca* is owned by a fabulous Belgian woman married to an Italian count."

"Aren't these *fincas* awfully old?" Susan asked him.

"Quite old, three-, four-, five-hundred years old, maybe a thousand. Or, *quién sabe*? There's a famous well called '*Pou des Lleo*' off the road to Cala Boix; it means 'Well of the Lion' in Catalan, but anthropologists say it was originally 'Well of the Legion,' as in Roman Legions."

The ma'moiselle labored up another steep, narrow path and Michael pointed across the shallow valley, "There . . . that's Led's *finca*, and it looks like he may be at home. The door seems to be open."

They Are Ruining Ibiza

The road tunneled through trees and eventually led to an opening in a whitewashed stone wall which surrounded a small courtyard. On one side of the courtyard were pens where farm animals had been kept, and an upper porch held empty dovecotes.

"Hey, this is like Santa Fe and Taos," Susan said.

The front door was open, and they went in. Several unfinished canvases were propped against the walls of the first room, which had a high ceiling and ran the length of the house.

Charles called, "Led . . . Ledyard . . . ." There was no answer.

"Didn't I tell you?" Charles said to Susan.

"Now, darling, it's another coincidence."

They searched the rooms, most of which had no windows or openings other than an entrance. One was a bedroom, with a rickety case of paperback books and outdated American magazines. Two small rooms were stacked with canvases in various stages of incompletion. One cubicle obviously functioned as a studio. The dark kitchen contained a huge fireplace across one end with an adobe platform above the opening. "Winter sleeping quarters," Michael said.

"I don't see any of the vulvas you were talking about," Susan said.

"He may have taken some paintings to Cuidad Ibiza. That's probably where he is."

A. C. Greene

"Then we'll have to wait here until he comes back, I suppose," Charles said.

Michael hesitated, "I don't know what to suggest. There's no way of knowing when he'll be back. He has friends around Ibiza town, and when he takes paintings in he often stays for a day or two."

"Where's the bathroom?" Susan asked.

"Take any pathway at the rear," Michael said.

"Good gosh, you mean there's no bathroom?"

"No bathroom, no running water, no electricity, no telephone."

"Did Christy live here?" Susan asked.

"Oh, yes."

"I can understand why she'd want to leave. No water, no bathroom, no telephone. No life for a lady."

"Water comes from the water company. You get used to living in terms of five-liter bottles. And they never charged Christy, she's such a charming *americana*. She acclimated quite nicely; marvelous cook, you know, does wonderful things with fresh fish and native dishes. The beautiful *sofrit pages* she makes have chicken, sausages, saffron, cinnamon, cloves in it."

Susan said, "Sounds marvelous . . . where may a tourist try it?"

"I'm afraid you can't find much Ibicenco food for sale today. Too complicated," Michael said, "a bit of *flao*, some *sobrasada* sausage, but no *sofrit pages*."

They Are Ruining Ibiza

Charles shook his head sadly, "Everything's ruining Ibiza."

❈❈❈❈

"Did I know or did I not?" Charles asked, after they returned to the hotel.

"You were right. But I still say it was a coincidence."

"Coincidence? Nonsense. There have been entirely too many for it to still be coincidence. Michael knew Led wasn't there. Couldn't you tell it?"

Susan frowned, "My God, Charles . . . why on earth would he have driven us all the way out there, over those horrible roads, if he knew nobody would be there when we arrived?"

Charles shook his head, "No, it was obvious to me that we were on a wild goose chase from the start; all that business about *el mercado* and that nonsense about Led now painting only vulvas. Did you see anything there, done or undone, that looked like a vulva?"

Susan laughed. "Charles, dear, we've already gone though our vulva routine . . . besides, I don't think I've ever heard of an undone vulva."

Charles snorted. "And another thing. Michael is in love with Christy. That's rather plain, too."

"Oh, Charles . . . just because Michael said Christy was a good cook."

A. C. Greene

"Believe me, I can tell. I'm surprised you couldn't. There was entirely too much admiration in Michael's voice as he so lovingly related what a noble creature she was, living out there in solitude, minus the amenities, and how superior was 'her' *sofrit* whatever."

"Charles, you *do* have to admire a modern woman who can survive under those awful conditions. Particularly an American girl. I damn sure couldn't. Or I wouldn't."

"And incidentally, *ma petite*, our worshipful guide is also attracted to you. Every time you slid out of that damned shoebox on wheels he had eyes for nothing but your knees, or whatever you chose to show."

"All right, Charles. I've already told you, I'm not going to dress like one of the old Ibicencas you admire so much. If you want a wife whose skirt sweeps the ground, go back to Es Pins and see if anything's available. As for Michael, he's sweet and unselfish, so naturally, you see it as conniving and lustful."

Charles tried to laugh, "Come on . . . you know I was teasing. My God, where's your sense of humor?"

"You're not teasing, Charles. You're acting like an old man; jealous, thinking everybody's trying to cheat you. Even your wife. Stop bugging me."

"'Stop bugging me.' Spoken like a child of the TV generation."

"I *am* a child of the TV generation. I can't help that. But nobody stays a child, particularly not my generation."

They Are Ruining Ibiza

Charles studied the floor for a moment, "I guess I act like an old man because life's making me an old man. As you say, I can't help it."

Susan moved to sit beside him on his bed. "I'm sorry," she whispered.

At that moment the house phone in their room whirred. Susan answered. It was Michael calling from the lobby. "I'm terribly sorry to break in on you like this, hope you were only napping; but could you two possibly join me for a quick drink, here at the lobby bar? It will only take moments."

"Just don't order a gin and tonic," Susan warned. Michael assured her, "My dear Mrs. Martyn, never order anything at an Ibicenco bar that calls for ice. They're worse than we Brits about ice. And we Brits may be coming out of it."

When they met him in the lobby, Michael said, "I feel rather badly about today, not finding Ledyard. I'd planned to see if you wanted to try Ibiza town tonight."

Charles said, "Forget it, Mike. We left Led detailed instructions out at the *finca* as to how to reach us. I'm sure we'll be hearing from him."

"Well, if I may beg off—Jonathan says an Austrian couple, heavy with schilling, have become enamoured of my painting and may wish to commission massive outlays if I meet them. I told Jonathan I was rather committed to you, but perhaps you could . . . ."

A. C. Greene

"I told you . . . forget it. We'll hear from Led, if not tonight certainly tomorrow."

"That could well be the case, unless he's staying in Ibiza for a few days," Michael said. "But whatever . . . I'll be back tomorrow, in case Led's still unsighted, and we'll search Ibiza town."

"Let's not worry about Led; let's have a drink and then you be off to waltz your Viennese."

Michael laughed loudly, "Oh, that's very good. Delightful."

When he and Susan returned to their room Charles shrugged, "Well, I guess we should have expected that. Michael's weary of the game, so he's opting out."

"I didn't take it that way at all," Susan said. "He's an artist. He has to make a living. And tomorrow, if Led's not turned up, he'll go with us to Ciudad Ibiza."

"You don't understand, darling. Michael will not be back, Led or no Led. Michael has played his role, he's done his part. We won't see him again."

"I can't accept that," she said.

"Have I been wrong yet?" he asked, then snorted, "Come on. Let's go to bed for a spell, then walk over to whatever that place is around the bay and have supper."

"It's *Sa Punta*, if you'd like to know the name."

Charles grinned, "I'd like something else better, right now."

❈❈❈❈

They Are Ruining Ibiza

That night, when they left the hotel, the moon was appearing, and Charles exclaimed, "One good thing about Spain: nothing ever closes. I heard music coming from Sa Punta at 2 A.M. Let's forget Led and all the goddamn progress that's ruining this island, and enjoy an evening by the sea, under the pines and the moon. I'm sure they'll play Rodrigo or de Falla. I might even be moved to compose bawdy limericks."

At *Sa Punta* the bathers and wind surfers were gone. Charles and Susan chose a table so near the sea that the waves came almost to their feet. Susan threw her head back and looked at the moon through their tree. "God, this is lovely," she said. "This romantic place, under a waxing moon . . . isn't that a waxing moon? . . . drinking San Miguel beer, eating these delicious little barbecued *tapas*."

"This is the way everything on Ibiza used to be," Charles said.

"Except for the music," Susan said. "Have you listened to what's coming from the loudspeakers? It isn't Rodrigo!"

Charles closed his eyes, "Damn . . . that's American music. Some rock outfit, isn't it?"

"Don't let it spoil the scene . . . I'm sorry I mentioned it. You hadn't even heard it."

"Oh, I had. It was nagging at my subconscious," he tapped his head. "I just wish there was some spot where a person could hide from it."

A waiter approached and asked if they wanted more drinks and Charles said they did. The waiter spoke rather good English and refused to return Charles' attempts to speak Spanish. Charles asked him why Sa Punta was recommended as a *playa* in the guide books but the beach was small and rocky.

"Much has changed," the waiter said. "The sea has been filled in. It once came there," he indicated a line behind the beach *kiosco* several yards from where they sat. "Our beautiful pine trees; ah, once they reached the shore. This is '*isla de pityusas*,' the Isle of Pines," he explained.

"*Pityusas* . . . is that Spanish?" Charles asked. "I thought pines was *pinos*."

"I do not know, sir," the waiter said, "but it is a very old name. Perhaps it is something no one understands anymore."

Charles laughed, "You hear a lot of that spoken nowadays."

It was well after midnight when he and Susan returned to the hotel. As they walked along the shore from *Sa Punta* the voice of Frank Sinatra pursued them softly through the dark. A note from Michael was in their box at the hotel's front desk. He said he would not be able to accompany them to Ibiza, as the Austrian couple wanted to see more of his work. The note said Sebastian, a friend of Led's, was happy to accompany them and would contact them tomorrow.

They Are Ruining Ibiza

"Here we go again," Charles said, flipping the note with his hand, "What did I tell you? Michael is passing the ball to Sebastian, whoever he is."

Susan interrupted, "Charles . . . why can't we wait until tomorrow to get upset about Sebastian?"

"This happens to be 'tomorrow.' It's 1:00 A.M."

"Oh, I didn't mean literally. But let's see what happens. We may be grateful for Sebastian's aid."

"Where does this Sebastian come in, anyway? Are we some kind of welfare clients the local citizens have to take turns with?"

"Well, we can't go searching the island on our own, looking for Led," Susan beckoned to her cot. "Here . . . if you'll come to bed right now I'll let you sleep with me."

"After this afternoon? What are you, a nympho?"

Susan giggled, "Don't tell me I'm taking advantage of you, Señor Mar-teen. One does not visit Ibiza solely to sunbathe."

Charles pretended to be stricken, "You are a nympho, aren't you?"

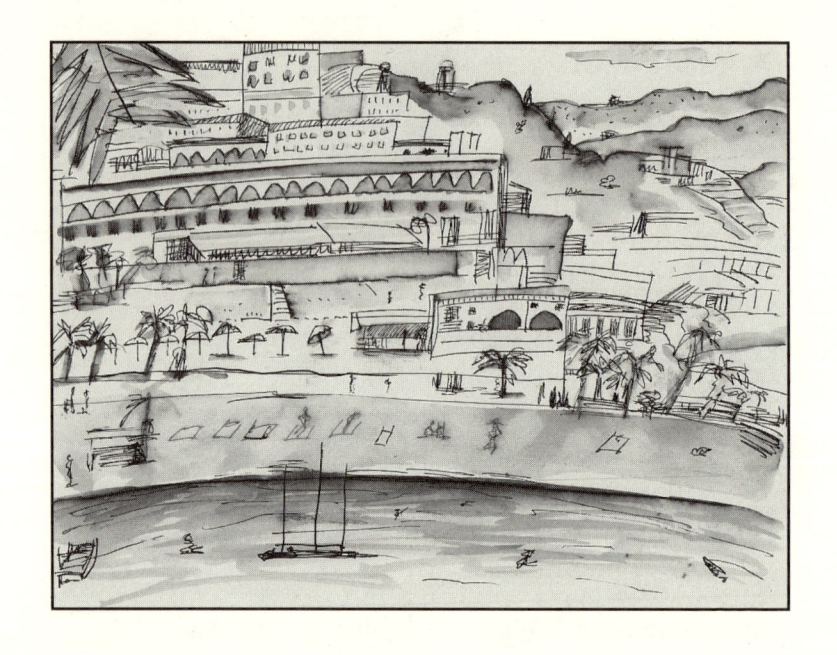

Five

The next morning they decided against breakfast in the dining room and chose instead to have *horchata* and *café con leche* on the hotel's sun-filled terrace. By mid-morning there had been no word of Led, so Charles walked down to the bay where the trucks were grinding away with their loads of rocks and the crane was steadily extending the breakwater. The yacht with the Texas flag was moored where it had been since they arrived, and this morning he could see no sign of life aboard except for the gaily waving flag.

They Are Ruining Ibiza

"Sons of bitches," Charles muttered.

He walked back to the hotel and Susan was in the lobby talking with a very handsome young man who appeared to be Spanish. She waved to Charles and he went to where they sat. The young man arose politely and Susan said, "Charles, this is Sebastian . . . Sebastian Santerre."

They shook hands and Sebastian said, "Michael asked that I inquire if you had found Led. As you have not found him, I offer my services, tonight also if you wish."

Charles asked, "You do know Ledyard, don't you?"

Sebastian nodded, "Quite well, but what is more important, I know where he hangs out."

Susan said, "Sebastian has offered to pick us up and take us to Ciudad Ibiza later this afternoon. I've already agreed. I want to see the town even if we can't find Led."

Sebastian smiled, "I feel sure we can do both, if that fits your plans?" He looked inquiringly at Charles, who shrugged and said, "My plans are . . . well, they depend on Led, so whatever you and Susan have cooked up . . ."

Susan shook her head, "Darling, we've cooked up nothing; we've been waiting for you."

Charles could see his remark upset her, so he shrugged again, "I will leave it entirely up to you two." He turned to Sebastian, "Shall I rent a car?"

Sebastian said, "Oh, no. I have a new Ford of which I am very proud."

They walked out to the hotel parking lot and saw the new automobile. Charles congratulated Sebastian on his good taste in body style and interior color but Sebastian admitted, sadly, that he had taken the only vehicle offered. "The Ford is *muy difícil* to obtain," he said, smiling. "One accepts what one is offered and goes on one's way rejoicing."

As they watched the automobile disappear, Charles said to Susan, "I don't suppose it's important that Sebastian is quite handsome and young?"

Susan pretended to consider, "Oh . . . well, yes, it *is* important. You see, Charles, this entire trip I've been looking for somebody young to occupy my time; not young enough to be my child, but quite young, and quite handsome. Surely you've noticed."

"I wasn't trying to be snide, darling. I just remarked that Sebastian is quite handsome."

"Well, then, let's get ready for Cuidad Ibiza," Susan said.

❄❄❄❄

Susan rode in the front seat with Sebastian and Charles felt a stir of resentment that she had chosen thus, although there was no way three adults could ride up front, and he certainly would not have forced Susan to ride by herself in the rear.

At Ciudad Ibiza Sebastian led them to a large outdoor cafe at the head of *Avenida Andenes*, the street that ran along the inner harbor. "This is as good a place as any," he said. "We can watch the strange ones, we will decide about

They Are Ruining Ibiza

the night, and we can find Led if he is in Ibiza, because sooner or later everyone must pass here."

They had a round of *café con leche* and Charles insisted they share *tapas*. "One is not obligated to order food," Sebastian advised them. "Many people sit for hours with one cup of *café con leche*."

"I want to see the old city and the fort or *castillo* or whatever it's called," Susan said, pointing to the heights above them.

"I am only too happy to escort you," Sebastian said, including Charles in his offer.

"Go on," Charles told them. "I've seen D'alt vila back when it really was an old town—oldest in Europe, they said."

"But darling . . . I wanted to see it with you," Susan said.

"Forget it. I'll wait here on the chance Led shows up. Go on. I insist."

Susan looked at Sebastian and he looked at Charles. "Very well," he said. "Mrs. Mar-teen and I shall go upward through the *portillo* and examine the heights."

"Oh, come now, Sebastian. I'm only 'Mrs. Martyn' to him," she smiled, nodding her head toward Charles.

❖❖❖❖

He watched the crowds passing up and down the waterfront, where a dozen or so outdoor places offered food, drink, shade or exposure, whichever was most important to the visitor. Charles studied the strollers, feeling older as he did, because there was no question, this was youth—European, African, Asian, American (he saw a few he thought might be *norteamericanos*) golden, bronze, olive, black youth . . . shockingly beautiful young humanity in every free-form of creation.

Was he too elderly, or too wise, to fall under the spell of Tanit, the Punic goddess of love, as that poster urged, over a shop a few meters down the *avenida*? His meditation was interrupted by a group which came tumbling and babbling into the open air cafe, clustered around a smallish man Charles recognized as a famous European film director whose name he could not remember. A stunning teenaged blonde, virtually sewn to his arm—Scandinavian or Polish, he would guess—seemed to be his primary escort, although there were two other stunning dark creatures among the director's intimate throng, eager to assume whatever role he might assign or they might, with luck, assume.

The ferry from Mallorca pulled in and a metallic gray Rolls Royce was first off the ship and, chauffeur-driven, proceeded down the dock toward the heart of Ibiza. As the magnificent vehicle progressed, dozens of arms and voices of those at the cafes were raised in salute to the owner, who waved, smiling and democratic, from the rear seat. Charles felt sure he was observing someone great of wealth (dope? electronics?) and small of brains. I doubt I'd care to

They Are Ruining Ibiza

know him, he thought to himself. I doubt I'd care to know any of these famous nonentities . . . except, damn it, he'd been moved by a couple of the films that director had made; the weaselly little bastard must have some sort of genius to get the performances out of those young actresses he was famous for keeping in his harem.

What the hell am I doing here, in the youth capital of Europe? Do I think because I have a young wife I'm young, too? Is there something that can be recaptured? Even my son is too young to understand an old father. Now, I am by myself, without the always-present need for armor, the need to keep the barb constantly at hand. Why? Was this visit to Ibiza to be a repetition of the other one? Was disaster the inevitable outcome of everything he did?

Oh, hell . . . why did he seduce himself with disaster? When and why did it start? He vaguely remembered a boyhood that was lived optimistically because it had to be. There was no other way for him to have climbed out of the pit birth had placed him in. So, was courting disaster, even when disaster was reluctant to be courted, his remission for guilt? Was it fear that always turned him toward the dark side of any "perhaps" that arose? After the optimism, where had the severe weather overtaken the caravan, to follow above it, a cloud full of ominous winds? Ominous: that was a word that carried satisfactorily descriptive tones for any occasion. Predicated on what? Life was ominous. Omen-ous. And what should one call all these coincidences, as Susan would have it? Omens?

A. C. Greene

Evil omens? Dismal augury. (What is the word for telling the future by reading ripped-out bird entrails?)

Dr. Charles Martyn, if you predict dark enough, will it always come true, or will the final event be lighter? To avoid disillusion, avoid illusion. To avoid unhappiness, avoid happiness? No, not even Dr. Martyn was that cynical. Oh, you self-applauding romantic, you defender of the unfaith. It cost you a wife, a good wife.

He had loved Harriet. The split, at her request: "I can't take it any more . . ." Some female should take out a patent on that phrase; men aren't allowed to use it. Omenous times turned ominous; voluntarily. Ask of yourself, Dr. Martyn, a true confession—there's no one else to hear, or ask. Did you start it deliberately? Do you believe God is listening, and if He is, do you believe He can do anything about it? Second paragraph: do you believe in God? Do you believe God? Do you believe?

Harriet had lost him somewhere along the way (Nat King Cole, 1952, Capitol Record, right?), and by then he had not only lost her, he'd lost Ledyard. Never an official break—no legal decree—but he'd never had him again like he'd had him when Led was a boy, six, eight, twelve years old. Did the evil omens of that first visit hang over Ibiza for this visit? Oh, hell! Stop that goddamn romanticism, that defending of yourself. This entire mental catharsis is nothing but a pretentious defense of yourself as a romantic. You've heard it too much, told yourself you are one too often. What you are is a first class prick, a schmuck.

They Are Ruining Ibiza

And even that grows to be a sort of joyous omen of disaster: I think prick, therefore prick am I.

Origin of word *schmuck*: Lloyd Himmelfarb Henry, who called him that in admiration. Poor Henry, killed crossing Route 5 at 1:00 A.M. while a Visiting Lecturer at Smith College. He was a handsome bastard, young enough to have thrilled the hearts of the Smithies. God . . . time takes its toll, doesn't it? Henry while young is an eternal Henry. "Henry While Young." Possible title for book? Fiction? Isn't it time you tried fiction, wrote a real book? How about "Susan While Young"? Sorry, old man, but that's nonfiction. The paperback rights would sell, with the right cover. Good film possibilities. But not a real book, you schmuck. What about Charles Martyn, by love possessed? Did she love him or possess him? The question must be asked, but he must never let himself ask it. Martyn never breaks.

I love, you love, he loves—could he love? Of course he could love. He had told Susan so, had meant it deeply and sincerely; had told her, as though confessing a sin, that she had discovered love for him; had begged her to, always, remember what he said, despite what his voice, his exterior, might exhibit. He had wished he could be an artist for once, not just a critic, so that it could be said in such a way that she would always remember and believe. The power of love. Hadn't they pledged, promised, vowed not to confess? But without suspicions. That may be one advantage of age-and-youth: neither thinks the other could possibly have sinned—one too old, the other too young. Forgiveness had never been a topic of their conversation.

So why did you send, insist on sending, her up into the old city, with that extraordinarily handsome young man? To test something, or prove it? Prove it to whom? That was obvious: to prove it to age. Schmuck . . . you want her to slip, don't you? That way, you won't have to answer that pestiferous question of why she married you in the first place, why she's stayed married to you, does she love you? Does she? Yes, even that would be answered if she, if she . . . God, don't think about it. Stop, right now. You're headed in the wrong direction, the compass needle is stuck. On north? On nothing. Pointing straight down. The lost patrol (with Victor McLaglen) marching forward or backward, it can't tell which.

❋❋❋❋

It took him a few seconds, in his musing, to realize someone was addressing him, someone besides his inner voice answering his own questions. "Martyn . . . I say, Dr. Martyn?"

A big man with a black and white beard was leaning over him, looking down with a defiant smile, "Isn't it Charles Martyn. Remember me? C. Harlan Smith? We were on a National Humanities panel at Yale when I was a graduate student. You got furious when Elkins failed to recognize your Hawthorne book. Remember?"

They Are Ruining Ibiza

The bearded man was wearing Nikes, old denims, and an orange T-shirt with a drawing of a female cat holding an electric vibrator and the message: "*Les Hommes Sont Tous Des Egoistes!*"

"Come on Martyn. Don't play coy. You know who I am."

Who in hell is this goddamn phoney? He's obviously looking for some kind of entree. "You'll have to forgive me, but I've been away from academe and haven't kept up . . ." Charles started to say ". . . with you young hot-shots" but the fellow didn't look young enough for the compliment.

The bearded man snarled. "I'm out of academics now, myself. Houghton-Mifflin turned down *Beaching the White Whale*. Doesn't that tell you anything?"

Humor the schmuck or face him off?

"I take it, then, you're not on sabbatical?"

"Fuck no. They couldn't pay me enough *pesetas* to stay in the university rat race. I'm through. Finis. I live here, on this island."

"I'm sure it's enjoyable," Charles said, wishing someone or something would distract this jerk.

"Hell yes, it's enjoyable, if you like to eat and fuck. Nobody goes hungry for food or pussy on Ibiza. And I'm thinking about busting things open back in the States. You'll hear about it if I do. From your cronies."

Charles remarked as superciliously as possible, "When a failed academic threatens, in that trite phrase, to 'bust things open,' it's nearly always a book. Which campus is your target? Not Yale, I hope; it seems to me Yale's been overdone. And am I to infer I'm not included in your . . . bust?"

"Why should I give you any more publicity?"

"But . . . surely you're not merely rewriting *The Bleached Whale* or whatever your title? *Moby Dick* is no longer open to second-guessing." No point in being polite to the creep.

"Fuck *Moby Dick*. And fuck you, Martyn. I burned that fucking manuscript. You elderly turds don't allow new opinions from 'jealous little second-raters' like me 'coming out of graduate school and flooding the state colleges,' as you put it."

"Look, Smith, if that's your name, I'm sorry your career went off the rails and I'm sorry I don't recognize you, but you have the wrong man in mind. That phrase you quoted was said by Nevin Schildkraut making fun of himself. And I can't recall being on a humanities panel at Yale in the past twenty years. As for Stanley Elkins overlooking my book, that is clearly a misconception. Elkins and I were friends before any of my ten books was published." There, that ought to move this hulking ignoramus along.

Smith glared for a moment, then growled, "Okay, Martyn . . . I guess you really don't know who I am. I'll give you a hint: we've both fucked the same woman."

They Are Ruining Ibiza

Good God . . . could Harriet possibly have made a connection with this . . . this, but . . . my God, it couldn't be . . .

"I'm Carl Harlan Smith, Susan's ex-husband. I thought she'd have told you what a son of a bitch I am, if nothing else." He seemed disappointed.

"Susan . . . my wife? She's never told me anything other than you married very young, had no children, divorced . . . ." Charles was shaking inside, and his voice was on the edge of cracking.

"I'm sorry, Martyn. I flattered myself that you knew all about me from Susan. I really was on a panel with you. And maybe it wasn't Elkins that acted like a prick about your book . . . maybe it was Leo Gannet. You ought to remember, he ripped you a new asshole."

"The late Leo Gannet? I hardly knew him. And why keep on about that Hawthorne book? It's out of print. Stick to the only subject we could possibly share interest in: Susan." Charles paused, "How did you recognize me if that was the only time you'd seen me? Somebody warned you. You didn't just stumble across me and remember back twenty years."

"No . . . I'd heard you were on Ibiza, you and Susan. I was curious. I guess I'm still a little jealous."

"Then that tale of the hedonistic academic is bullshit."

Smith shook his head sadly, "Nope . . . that's not bullshit. I'm here, living on the island. Going to seed. When I found out you and Susan were on Ibiza I knew you'd get to the city sooner or later, and I thought I might . . ." he paused, "get a glimpse of Susan."

"Well, you missed her. She's gone to D'alt vila . . . with a fellow from Santa Eulalia named Sebastian. You've seen me, you played your little game, and I don't want you around when they come back here."

"I know Sebastian. Everybody knows Sebastian. You live here and you know everybody. Too goddamn well."

"And Sebastian couldn't wait to phone you we were on our way."

Smith shook his head, "Pure coincidence. I just happened to stroll off Paseo Vara del Rey and suddenly, there you were: you, Sebastian . . . and I saw Susan. But I'm civilized enough so that I waited until she left to face you."

Charles scoffed, "Bullshit . . . Sebastian set it up. He gave you our estimated time of arrival, then he sweet-talked Susan into seeing D'alt vila and sweet-talked me into staying here so you could come rub it in."

"Rub it in? Jesus Christ! Rub what in and on whom? You think if things had been set up I would have wanted to talk to you and not Susan? It was a coincidence."

"There've been too goddamn many coincidences. This whole trip of ours has been a coincidence. It doesn't make me a damn that you'd want to gaze your fucking heart out at my wife, but I'm not stupid enough to think this is a coincidence. Who told you we were on Ibiza? If it wasn't Sebastian, who was it? Michael? Jonathan? The English broad at Es Moli?"

They Are Ruining Ibiza

"It was Led. He told me you were coming."

"So he got my cables, and that's why everyone's been playing games with us. Do they think if Susan sees you again she'll desert her elderly spouse?"

"Damn it, I don't know anything about games. I haven't seen Led in two weeks, maybe longer. And I don't expect you to believe me, but I did wait until Susan left to come here . . . and I don't want to be here when she comes back. Seeing you was a coincidence, coming to face you was an impulse."

"I don't believe a word of it," Charles said.

"And one other thing; Led doesn't need you spoiling things for him."

"Don't try to read my intentions."

"Maybe he doesn't want you to find him. Maybe he's happy, maybe you represent something he doesn't want to face. Maybe you should catch the first plane back to the States and wait 'til he decides to show up over there."

"And maybe I know my son better than you do, 'Doctor' Smith . . . just as I know Susan better."

"But you don't know Ibiza. Have you read the history of this damn island? Ibiza is dangerous. This is a place for wrecks—where they wash ashore; this is where bottles from all over the world float in with meaningless messages."

"That's romantic hogwash; an excuse somebody like you offers himself for his lack of success. You've never won a match, have you 'Doctor' Smith? You've lost every set you've played."

Smith said slowly, "If you weren't so much older than me, I'd kick your butt."

"And that would solve things, wouldn't it? Kick my butt and your troubles are over. That would publish that ridiculous book for you, make you a full professor . . . get Susan back, wouldn't it?"

Smith shook his head, "Leave Susan out of this; I left her out. You do likewise."

"How can we leave Susan out when she's the only possible excuse I would have for tolerating even five minutes of your nonsense? Get this through your head: she loathes you. There was nothing in that marriage for her but frustration and dismay, if that's not too kind a way to describe how she felt."

"You don't know your ass about that marriage and I'm not so sure you know as much about Susan as you think you do. She ever tell you how good we were in bed? She was crazy for it. She ever describe some of the little tricks she used? I'll bet you a goddamn seven-course dinner at San Telmo she's never used 'em on you. Or are you too old to enjoy that kind of thing? So don't try to tell me about Susan. It's a subject I'm better at than . . . . "

"You weren't very good at it. You couldn't keep her. She walked out on you. She's told me all about it."

Carl Smith looked at Charles with hostility. "You said you'd never discussed our marriage, you son of a bitch."

They Are Ruining Ibiza

Charles sneered. "She got tired of your whining and walked out on you. She couldn't take any more. I know all about that."

"She walked out on me? No, dear Dr. Martyn. I kicked her out. I was the one who couldn't take any more." Smith looked away from Charles but continued to speak, softly, "God . . . the first one I caught her with was Elzie . . . good old Elzie Weckler. My office mate at Cortland. Jesus, I couldn't believe it. She cried and Elzie said he'd resign if I wanted him to . . . and I forgave 'em. Poor fool me. Then it was Rhys Briggs, the great Welsh show-off, screwing every faculty wife on campus. I didn't think about him screwing mine. Somewhere in there was Rozik, the Hungarian physicist, or Gustav Herman . . . she loves Europeans, in case you haven't had the chance to observe. And after a while I gave up. I didn't try to find out . . . I didn't have to try; she told me about it in great detail. It turned her on, telling me about the men she'd fucked while she fucked me. I even got to liking it . . . but I couldn't take it. Walking across the campus, I wanted to kill every man I met. Finally I threw her out. Then I threw myself out . . . and gave up everything."

Charles was panting, trying to catch his breath. "It's . . . a lie. A goddamn lie. You're making it up."

"Of course it's a damn lie . . . because you want it to be, because it has to be, doesn't it? A damn lie to protect your old age and what's left of your manhood. Susan's about all that's left of your manhood, isn't she? Pretty little

Susan. Safe and sweet, loving and gentle. Telling her old husband what a stud he is. Letting him fool himself that he satisfies her . . . keeping everything on schedule; giving him a hard-on one or two times a week . . . going to bed with him when she can't put it off any longer . . . ."

"Shut up! Hear me? Shut up! You're a filthy bastard. Susan loves me and I love her. Nothing else counts. Nothing." Charles was half out of his chair; only the heavy metal table kept him from slashing out at Carl Smith.

The younger man waved a hand at him. "Sit down . . . you're just making a bigger fool of yourself; I'm not some graduate student who has to kiss your ass for a degree," Smith sneered.

"Kick my ass, then! Make me sit down! Try it . . . come on. Don't let my age stop you . . . ."

Smith shook his head, "It's not your age that stops me, it's my civilization. By God, living on Ibiza has made me more civilized than you."

Charles was on his feet, then a shaking, a wave of weakness swept over him and he wavered, barely upright. "Get out of my sight," he pleaded with the younger man. "Just get out of my sight."

Carl Smith hesitated, almost apologetic. "I didn't come here to hurt anybody. Not Susan. Not even you. But I told you not to make me mad. To leave Susan out of it. I'm human, goddamit. You can't expect me not to defend myself. Why should I be cast as villain when I was anything but? Susan was the one. She caused everything."

They Are Ruining Ibiza

Charles shook his head fiercely, "Shut up and go away . . . you haven't hurt me. Don't flatter yourself. You think anything you could tell would have the slightest effect on Susan and me? The way I feel about her? You're an insufferable shit."

Smith cut in desperately, "And you're a phoney, a fraud. You've got to live with the knowledge that you're a broken down academic with a one-book reputation. That's all that's left to you."

"But who got her? I got her . . . and who lost her? You lost her; you live with that." Charles's words could barely be heard, but he was smiling, "Now fuck off."

Smith hesitated, started to say something else. Charles motioned him away, gesturing with the back of his right hand and averting his eyes so he would not have to look at the younger man again. Carl Harlan Smith turned without another word and moved through the tables toward the Paseo de Rey without glancing back.

❉❉❉❉

Charles slumped in the metal chair, not counting time or seeing the colorful parade around him. Jesus God, what was happening? Why was he running over that list of lies, checking points . . . finding parallels. Stop it, for God's sake . . . for your own sake. She's yours. She loves you . . . she's satisfied. What difference does anything else make? Even if you believed the son of a bitch . . . and you don't

A. C. Greene

believe that crap, do you? No, God no! But the parallels. Those little points which intrigue the second-self, the *doppelgänger*, that alert the *wyrd* that forever sits on your shoulder pecking life to pieces. Don't get symbolism mixed up in this. You no more believe in *wyrds* and *doppelgängers* than you do mermaids . . .

It's coincidence; life is coincidence. Accept that. But it's tough, what life continues to do with coincidence, like letting that bastard be on Ibiza. Coincidence that he knew those points, those parallels? Lies can coincide with reality; goddamn it, lies can be truthful without knowing it. Everything he said about her was a lie. And a broken down academic, a one-book reputation . . . more lies. Everything he said about everything was a lie. That's another goddamn myth of the young, that they see truth through new eyes and face it fearlessly. Bull shit! What is truth, what are new eyes, and who is fearless?

There was a conspiracy, a conspiracy by life . . . not to defeat him but to shut him out, bottle him up, isolate him; keep him uncertain. To put him on an island where, even in independence, he cannot handle fate, cannot outrun his *wyrd*. Goddamn it, don't fall back into your *wyrd* crap. You were nineteen years old when you studied that Anglo-Saxon fate . . . or was it Norse? Old Dr. Hattie Watson taught you that. She didn't believe it, but you did. I've outgrown it, for God's sake. But why is everything always turning wrong? What road not taken was the one that would have led out of the yellow wood? Robert Frost,

They Are Ruining Ibiza

you smug bastard . . . "I took the one less traveled by . . ." How the hell did you know, if you never went back and tried the other one? All your goddamn poetry is smug. "Whose woods these are I think I know . . ." Never taught Frost my whole damn career.

Jesus, Susan, why did you ever get connected with him . . . with them. Susan, why did you? Didn't you know what he was, couldn't you see how it was bound to turn out? Why couldn't somebody have told you to wait for me—when you were twelve years old?

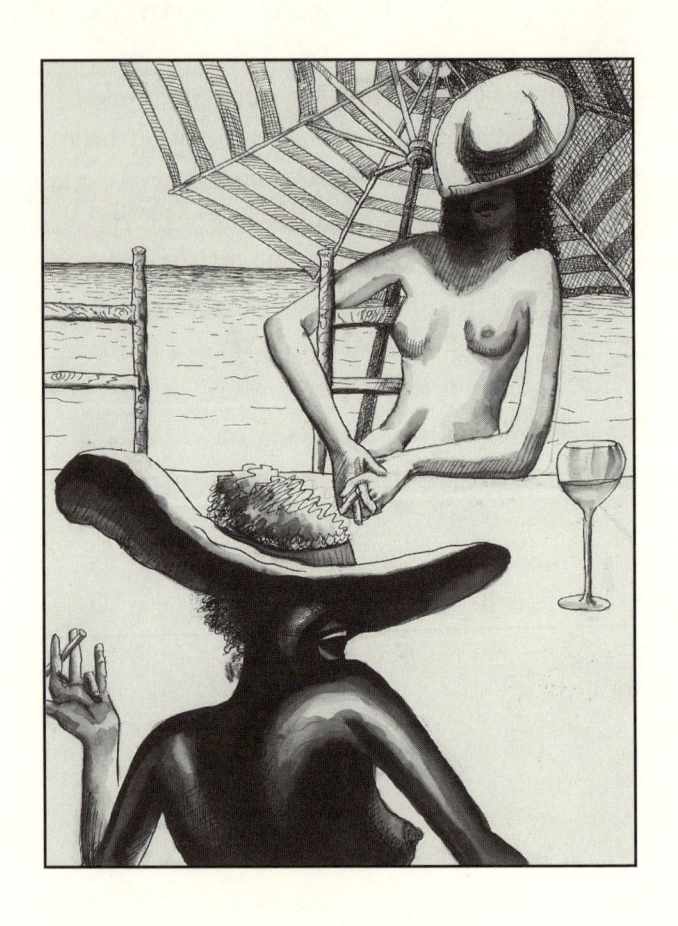

Six

"Are you asleep, darling?" Susan was beside his chair, Sebastian with her. It was almost dark. She smiled when he looked up. "We had the most wonderful little trip; the view from up at the fort is staggering, the stone walls and those narrow little stinky streets so . . . so *ancient*; they

They Are Ruining Ibiza

smell like urine, but they're so romantic. I got down on both knees and felt of part of the wall that Sebastian told me was Roman. And up at the top just now, the sun going down and the lights coming on one at a time: pop! pop! pop! and a big cruise ship out on the Mediterranean, all white and lighted . . . I wished you were with us."

Charles smiled dazedly, "Fine, darling. I enjoyed my . . . recess."

"Admit it, you slept, didn't you?" Susan smiled.

Charles nodded. "I said, I enjoyed my recess. It gave me time to reflect on the ways of mankind . . . and (he winked) womankind. I admit, I observed my fellow humans through slightly lowered lids, but I sat straight up and napped without getting caught, like I learned to do in church when I was a boy. But slept? Never! I'm ready to eat."

Sebastian laughed, "Then I suggest we have supper at El Corsario, up in D'alt vila. It's above the crowd and has a marvelous view of the sea."

Charles pursed his lips, "I've been there. When I was here before, and I don't want to go back to anything . . . ."

"I understand, of course," Sebastian said, "then shall we go to *El Sausalito*, at the breakwater? Everyone famous must eat at *El Sausalito* to be seen of themselves or to see who comes and goes. I can guarantee at least one prince, possibly the race driver Vini Loupe, or Cassillo, our famous Spanish tenor . . . and marvelous seafood."

A. C. Greene

Susan took Sebastian's arm, "Hurry . . . we may miss that in-crowd. Besides, I'm famished." She looked up at Charles and asked, quietly, "You're all right, aren't you? You have that look on your face. Did something happen?"

"I'm perfectly all right. I guess I dozed a bit too long. You know how daytime sleep does me."

Sebastian smiled, "But, before we go to *El Sausalito* . . . may I beg a few moments away to conduct a personal matter? I shall be gone only a short while."

"Of course," Susan said, and Charles shrugged, "Certainly."

After Sebastian left them, Susan said, "He must be needing to use the restroom. He's too shy to come right out and say so."

"Restroom, hell. He's going off to use the telephone, out of our hearing."

Susan agreed, "Well, that might also be true. He does have a private life."

"Getting the cast ready for the next act."

"Oh, dear, Charles . . . are you back on that again?"

"I don't trust him. He's in cahoots with them."

"In cahoots? Who with . . . with whom?"

"I just don't trust him, and I have good reasons."

Susan frowned, "But who do you think he's in cahoots with, Charles? You don't even know him. You don't even know anybody who knows him except Michael."

"Everybody on Ibiza knows Sebastian. Hasn't he told you?"

They Are Ruining Ibiza

Susan peered at him with concern. "Darling, I hope you're tipsy. Otherwise . . . well, what has come over you? You haven't been sitting here drinking and brooding all afternoon, have you?"

"Do I look like I've been drinking all afternoon?"

"No . . . but you're acting like you have."

"Listen . . . I'm not imagining anything about Sebastian . . . oh, here he comes."

Sebastian, smiling, said, "I'm so sorry I had to leave you. But now everything is taken care of and we must proceed to *El Sausalito*."

"Did you make your phone call?" Charles asked. Sebastian looked confused. Susan took Sebastian's arm, "Hurry."

She looked back at her husband knowingly, "I do hope you can overcome your momentary lagging of spirits."

"I'm perfectly all right." Seeing her, realizing and now accepting how dependent he was on her, he was suddenly torn between wanting to hurt her and wanting to make love to her right here, now—but afraid even to touch her, afraid she might cry out, or cringe.

❈❈❈❈

Sebastian was saying, "Our nights, on Ibiza . . . they do not truly begin until three or four hours from now. Then, shall we go to Club *¿Cual?*" Sebastian pronounced "club" as "cloob." He paused and frowned at Charles, "It is the most important on Ibiza right now. Do you wish to find your son Ledyard?"

Charles said slowly, "Yes . . . I wish to find Ledyard. Why?"

"It is most possible he might be at Club *¿Cual?*."

Charles frowned, "Doesn't *cual* mean 'which'? Is it that kind of club?"

"It is a very amusing place," Sebastian said. "You may do whatever you please. That is why it is named '*Cual.*'"

❀❀❀❀

Do you wish to find your son Ledyard? Of course. Wasn't that why they had come to Ibiza, to find his son? But the search had not begun here on Ibiza; it was old by now. He had been searching for Ledyard for years—and Ledyard had probably been searching for him. They met, yes, but finding one another was something else. And the search continued. Neither able to do whatever it might take to discover the other.

Fathers and sons . . . were they all like this? His own father had become a stranger by the time Charles was Led's age. No enmity between them, only bafflement. They had so little to share by then: Charles had a world into which he had fitted himself, into which he had forced his way—like putting on a pair of tight boots. He had created a tunnel which allowed him through the wall without using the gate. He had had to do it that way. He

They Are Ruining Ibiza

didn't have the keys that allowed most of his colleagues to use the locked gate. They had all fought him: hadn't liked his dissertation, hadn't liked his published criticism; "too personal," "too subjective." The journals tried to trivialize him: "popularizer." But like they used to say about Liberace, that piano player who kept a tacky candelabra on his piano—he laughed all the way to the bank.

A one-book reputation? Perhaps. But it freed him from having to be too concerned with what the guild thought . . . but long since he'd become part of the guild, too. It was inevitable, if you succeeded. If you whipped them at their game it became your game, too. And Charles Martyn had bitterly wanted success . . . not just fame or the magnificent economics of success, but the kind that made you doubly independent, kept you protected from caring what the bastards said or what they did. Their gossip, their nasty reviews in the journals . . . you had succeeded. Your reputation was secure. They could argue with you but they couldn't disregard you. ("But you let them keep you fighting after you won the war," Harriet had told him.)

What was this uncontrollable compulsion that ruled him? To get, to climb, to achieve, to seize happiness, to grab it whether it wanted to be grabbed or not. He hadn't been ignorant, that man his father; he was not without his own hopes and desires . . . but he was too easily contented for the young Charles Martyn, and that part of the son never changed. Did not bend or break.

A. C. Greene

His father had never wanted to be any place but where he was, literally and figuratively. Excitement came hard to the old man. The old man? You never called him that in your life; never saw him that way. (What way did you see him? What way does Led see you? Does Led see you at all?)

Fathers and sons. Maybe they should have had more children, he and Harriet. Why had they not? He couldn't remember every obstacle, except that one: money. When that was less of an obstacle, it was too late. Not biologically too late, but too late for what the life they had come to live was centered around: not the child or children . . . but Dr. Charles Martyn. It had to be that way. There is no competition fiercer than that on campus, and none, within that little realm of inflated egos and reputations, is more barbarous than among those with critical textbooks on the market. And he had been an academic Ishmael; a wild ass of a man, his hand against every man and every man's hand against him . . . .

❈❈❈❈

They got to *El Sausalito* and were seated at a table that looked out over the mouth of the harbor and the little lighthouse that flashed its lonely candle at the end of a long jetty. "Perfect," Susan said, and Sebastian smiled in gratitude, like a child. But where are the princes and the opera singers you promised? Charles could not keep himself from covert glances around the large room.

They Are Ruining Ibiza

Sebastian, as if reading his thoughts, began apologizing, "Oh, Pro-fess-or Mar-teen . . . I have failed you. There are no princes or racing car drivers, I fear. You are the most famous man in the room."

Susan smiled and reached over to pat her husband on the cheek. "He's right, Charles. Your obvious importance hovers like a cloud about our table."

"Let's eat," Charles said. "Hunger makes me infamous."

Seven

They left the city and suddenly were plunged into the Ibicenco night. The countryside they drove through looked empty, without shadows, soft and blue. Club ¿*Cual?* was located on a hill deep in the island's interior off the road between Ibiza and San Antonio de Abad. It shone, a lighted pearl on the dark landscape.

They Are Ruining Ibiza

As they approached the club by way of a swaying bridge above a pool lit by underwater lights, the beating of the music began taking away every other sound. Sebastian flashed a key, which hung around his neck, and they were admitted by a tall, dark doorman who never said a word—but with a sweep of the arm passed them on. Charles noticed three other couples waiting, looking around hesitantly, as if they might discover something unexpectedly magic, out there in the dark, that would miraculously deliver proof they were worthy of admission.

Sound came booming from invisible speakers atop tall towers and was audible long before they got inside the club. Perhaps, with the right wind, it could carry from one shore to the other. Inside Club *¿Cual?* was a swirling ten-thousand square meters of laser-lighted roar, driving through a collection of tents, pavilions and awnings of white silky fabric before soaring into the dark. Tall palms and ominous looking plants poised to reach out and capture the dancers and lovers swooping and gliding among them. The pounding beat and dizzying light effects whipped the crowd into frenzied, deranged response.

"Everyone in this place must be insane if they are here every night," Charles said.

Sebastian smiled, "Many are. Others become insane after they arrive."

Club *¿Cual?* was a madhouse with inmates garbed, or half-garbed, in outlandish, glittery, nonsensical wrappings; tinsel and plastic, daubed with paint, lipstick, sequins.

A. C. Greene

Almost every female had bared her breasts, and the female-looking persons who had not were immediately suspect of not being female.

As they went toward their table, Susan said, "Let's dance." She grabbed Charles's arm and swung him toward what seemed to be the dance floor, a runway that passed across a pool of water, circling to form a continuous parade of slithering, rocking figures, played over by bursts of laser light.

"I'm overdressed for this zoo," Charles said. "Some of the animals don't have a stitch on."

"Take off your shirt, then."

"I'd fit in better taking off my pants."

"Well, take off your pants, but come on and dance," she smiled. "Isn't that cute . . . a poem: Take off your pants, but come on and dance." She shook his shoulder. "Turn loose, Charles. Be somebody else for a while," Susan patted his cheek. "You're a very sexy man, believe me."

"I can't believe anything in a place like this," he said. "Everything's fantasy. Everything's 'which?'" A beautiful blonde passed by wearing silvery pasties on her nipples and an intricately beaded G-string with heavy strands of matching jewels around her neck. Two men, their green hair cropped short, no clothing but green velvet breech clouts, their bodies dyed green from head to foot, danced slowly across the water, circling and twirling to every fourth or fifth beat of the savage music.

They Are Ruining Ibiza

After they were seated, a male waiter, wearing a colorless plastic apron, a barely visible jock strap, and black jack boots, asked for their drink order.

"*Un poco loco*," exclaimed Sebastien.

"Me, too," Susan said, "*dos poco locos*."

The waiter looked at Charles, "*Y Vd., señor? Lo mismo?*"

"Have a *poco loco*," Susan begged. "Please, just once."

"*Cerveza* San Miguel," Charles told the waiter.

"*Sí, señor*," the young man said. As he departed Charles could see, through the plastic apron, a bluish mark on one buttock; teeth prints of a human bite. "My God, look at that," he whispered to Sebastian and Susan. "That fag's lover bit him in a moment of passion."

Sebastian laughed. "That is a tattoo, my friend. In Cala Llonga is a marvelous artist of tattoo." Sebastian rose to his feet and bowed. "My friends, may I once more attend to something personal, *un momento, por favor?*"

Sebastian disappeared into the swirl. "There he goes again," Charles said.

"Forget Sebastian for a while," Susan begged. "Don't get paranoid. You're here to have fun, be reckless—remember?" She leaned over and embraced him. "Sweetheart, for once, give in. I've been waiting years for you to be yourself. You're not in New York, you're not in Boston. You're in Ibiza and who knows who you are?"

He stopped himself from saying that someone always knows who you are, saying instead: "I'm not interested in whether anyone knows who I am . . . but I have some consideration for . . ." he started to say, "my age," but hesitated. "This . . . this *ambience*," he gestured, "urges something I have resisted all my life, something I have tried to teach a generation to resist . . . loss of control, surrendering reality to fantasy—giving it all up."

Susan smiled, "But that's why people come to Ibiza . . . to give it up. To be free of themselves. Sweetheart, that's your trouble, you're not free of yourself. You're not willing to give up anything. . ." she paused, shrugged, put a hand on his arm and smiled. "With or without you, darling, I'm going to dance."

"With whom?"

"If I can find him, with Sebastian. With someone else, if not. Or with myself. I just want to move."

"How cozy . . . and how convenient."

"Charles! Don't you understand . . . Sebastian's gay."

"Why do you say that?"

"Because it's . . . it's obvious. We haven't discussed it, but he takes for granted that we understand."

"Go on and dance. I don't give a damn who with. Get out there and flop your thirty-six-year-old tits and ass for the twenty-year-old crowd."

Susan glared at Charles. "All right, stay uptight. Keep yourself a prisoner . . . you're good at it. I'm not." She stopped. There were tears in her eyes. "Why are we always fighting, Charles? Are you at war with somebody? With me? Your ex-wife? Your son? Or is it yourself? Why? Why?"

They Are Ruining Ibiza

She watched him for a moment as he scowled, but did not answer. Then as she danced her way, alone, onto the runway, she unbuttoned her blouse, unhooked her bra, shook loose her breasts, and was immediately caught into and disappeared with a cloud of half-nude dancers revolving around her, and only now and then could he get a glimpse of her, breasts bouncing to the fierce music, sliding along the dancing circle on the other side of the pool.

The huge courtyard was surrounded by terraces where tables were placed. Waves of brilliant light swept around the gathering, followed immediately by blue darkness before light would burst back again. The music never stopped, never seemed to change, never slowed or grew quieter; it was a vast presence, more solid than the trees or the towers from which it poured—or the people it poured over. It was the clothing of the night.

❅❅❅❅

Sebastian appeared and asked, "Where is Señorita Susan?"

Charles nodded toward the line of dancers, parts of which were hidden by the pavilions and palm trees. "Somewhere 'mongst the madding crowd, shaking her tits and wiggling her ass like *una puta*."

Sebastian was shocked, "Dr. Martyn, do not say such a thing. Susan is a wonderful person, not a *puta*. Is it I toward whom you are so angry? Should I not have brought you here?"

What the hell's happening to me? Am I going crazy? Take hold. "Oh, hell, Sebastian . . . forgive me for calling Susan a whore. I'm not angry at you . . . or anyone. I'm . . . I'm *al revés*, turned inside out like a coat; a coat I've put on wrong."

Sebastian brightened, "Ah, you are *al revés!* Perhaps *un poco loco* instead of *cerveza* would make things *a derechas*."

Charles nodded, "Make things right? Okay, I'll have a *poco loco*. Where's a waiter?"

"I'll get it myself," Sebastian insisted. He dashed off into the crowd returning shortly with the drink, which seemed to be contained in half a coconut shell. He sat at the table with Charles, and Charles, raising his drink, shouted, "To you, Sebastian. To your skill and daring as a *bailador*; go find our lady and dance with her . . . dance until the sky drops or her panties drop, or I drop from *pocos locos* . . . ."

Sebastian jumped to his feet and laughed, "Ah, yes! And then, you will dance, perhaps?"

Charles brushed the thought away with a gesture, "Go on . . . go on, I'm an inside-out coat."

He sipped the strong tasty drink, discovering the coconut shell was plastic. He looked at the container in his hand, shook his head and exclaimed, "Shit."

Half a dozen times Susan danced by, once breaking out of line to toss her blouse and bra on their table, her

They Are Ruining Ibiza

breasts swaying attractively. Once she and a tall, Turkish-appearing man passed by, dancing in close embrace, her breasts crushed against his hairy chest. Charles closed his eyes and felt a shiver up his spine and across his shoulders. Some of the women had removed their skirts and were dancing in the scanty panties only the firm could afford to display. A Swedish girl, falling off the runway where it crossed the pool, caused the crowd to cheer when she emerged from the water and calmly flung away her wet underwear to rejoin the dancers.

A waiter came by Charles's table and winked, pointing to the drink, "*Poco mas?*" Charles smiled, "*Sí.*"

"*Está la hora borracha,*" the waiter said.

"It's the drunk hour, all right," Charles muttered agreeably, "whatever the time is. It is now the drunk hour all over España. All over the world."

A man and woman, dancing, both wearing only the slightest kind of string bottoms, circled each other at the top of the runway over the water, and began bumping pubic areas, holding their hands high; circling, bumping, circling, bumping, and rhythmically the man bent his head, attempting to catch a nipple in his mouth, with the onlookers clapping in time to his attempts.

Charles holding a third *poco loco* . . . sat listening to the voices around him, coming from out of the night: *la hora borracha:*

". . . an extremely fat Englishman tried to blow up a kiddie float . . . the puffing killed him."

A. C. Greene

"Of course it did, I know just the one you mean."

The voices began echoing, "Willie told Frederick, he's Greek, y'know, 'Ye've lost love (love . . . love) . . . ye don't even love ye'self anymore . . . (anymore . . . anymore)."

Who are they trying to provoke with that echo chamber? "I, Gary Cooper, I no provoke," Charles muttered, shaking his head. "Wrong actor. 'I, Akim Tamiroff, I no provoke.'" But he didn't like that name. That wasn't who he was. He was Gary Cooper, the brave American. "I, Gary Cooper," he said aloud, "I no provoke." Two heads turned in his direction and smiled.

He tried to focus on the provokers, but all he could see were dancers, turning like a wheel in his sight, up, around, and back down from the gauzy heights, weaving heads, feet, breasts, dark triangles of hair appearing, disappearing, where faces should be, the dancing wheel tumbling and spinning with the breasts all in a row . . . moving together . . .

"Charles . . . Charles, are you all right?"

The wheel slowed, the dancers ceased touching the gauze, the patches of pubic hair became faces.

"Susan," he turned, one finger on his lips, "Listen. They're talking to me, trying to provoke me . . . ."

Susan smiled at Sebastian, "How many beers has he had, do you suppose?"

Sebastian shook his head ruefully, "I am so guilty. I proposed he change to *poco locos* . . . he said he felt like he

They Are Ruining Ibiza

was turned inside out, *al revés*, so I suggested *poco loco* in place of *cerveza*. I should not have left."

Charles shook a denial, "I'm not drunk. I am listening to them. They are trying to provoke me, it's coming from up there in the dark . . . but I no provoke. You understand, I no provoke."

He touched Susan, caressing a breast. She took his hand away, "Mustn't do that, dear. It's not nice in public."

"That Turk was doing it," he told her. "I saw him . . . right up against you, mashing your titties against his big hairy chest. I saw him."

"We were dancing, darling. He wasn't caressing me. We were just dancing."

Charles looked around the table, "Where's your blouse? You'll freeze your pretties."

Susan laughed and held his hand, "I don't need a blouse. Nobody's wearing her blouse. See? I feel wonderful. I feel . . . me. I'm free of whoever that woman is who keeps butting into my life. I'm excited at being me." She turned to Sebastian, "Sebastian, sweetheart, if I were a few years younger I'd take off my skirt, too. I'd take off everything!"

Sebastian smiled, "Beauty observes no birthdays, Señorita Susan."

Now, on the dance path, the other dancers had drawn back, leaving one couple alone at the top of the arch over the pool. The couple danced, swirled, then began a series

A. C. Greene

of embraces, fondling, probing, the woman sliding to her knees as the man twisted suggestively.

Charles grabbed Susan's arm and pulled her around so she could see.

"What are they doing," he demanded, his drunkenness overcome for the moment. "What in God's name are they doing?"

She tried to see more clearly. "It looks like they're dancing."

"Dancing? Like hell. They're about to copulate. No! . . . Jesus! Look at the girl. I think she's going down on him, right there on the dance floor."

Susan put an arm around his shoulder and drew him to her, whispering in his ear, "Charles, please . . . don't yell; it's just an act." The crowd was cheering and whistling, the music never stopped . . . the thick, battering pulse of the crowd.

Sebastian leaned toward him and said, "There is Ledyard."

"Ledyard? Where is Ledyard? Don't tell me we've finally found him."

"See that girl?"

"Girl? Where?"

"The girl on the dance floor; she is not a girl. He's in drag . . . dressed like a woman."

"Yes, goddamn it, I know what drag means . . . but where's Led?"

"I told you. The girl, the woman. That is Ledyard."

They Are Ruining Ibiza

"Oh, my God . . . my God. . . ."

"What's wrong? What's the matter, darling?" Susan clutched his arm.

He flung his arm roughly from her grasp.

"Leave me alone, goddamn it. . . . leave me alone." He turned to Sebastian, "Why did you bring me here? Why?"

"But . . . sir . . . you wanted to find Ledyard . . . I thought you knew."

"The hell you did. All of you knew. Everyone but me." He growled savagely at Susan, "When did you find out, you scheming little bitch . . . I suppose you'll also tell me he has AIDS?"

"Don't, Charles . . . don't do this to us. You know better than that. I don't know what to say. I truly don't, except that . . . it's Led's choice. His life. Surely you understand enough to . . . ."

Charles turned on Sebastian, "Goddamn it . . . you knew when you brought me here that this is what I'd find, didn't you?"

Sebastian was near tears, "I . . . I did only what Ledyard himself asked, Señor Martyn. He wanted you to know but was afraid." Sebastian paused, "You are a man of today, a modern man, Señor Martyn. And what is so terrible about Led?" He looked steadily at Charles. "Or me?"

Charles shook his head violently. "I don't want to see him. I don't ever want to see him. I don't want to see anybody. I want to leave this goddamn island."

A. C. Greene

He stood up, holding onto a chair and waving his hand over the crowd: "They've all known, ever since we got to Ibiza. Protecting him; don't let his father find out . . . coincidence . . . shit!" He turned to the tables around them, and screamed "SHIT ON YOU!"

The music poured over them. At nearby tables a few faces turned, some smiling, one man yelling in approval, "*La mierda . . . mierda!*" Others took up the cry, laughing and pounding on the tables in rhythm, "*Mierda . . . mierda . . . mierda!*"

Charles swayed back from the sound, lurching away from where Susan and Sebastian had risen to their feet. Susan cried out, "Charles . . . darling; where are you going? . . . Wait!"

He ran, as much as his condition allowed, through the tables, pushing aside the dancers, across the bridge, stumbling toward the entrance, falling twice. Susan ran to him, "Charles . . . don't go."

He grabbed her roughly, "He can't do this to me!"

Susan shook her head, pleading, "He's not doing it to you, Charles. You're doing it to him."

The dark doorman watched with interest but did nothing to halt or help. Susan, calling his name, followed Charles, but when she reached the outer doorway the doorman refused to allow her to leave. He tried to explain in halting English, because she was *desnudo* it was *ilicito*. As she protested and continued calling, Charles reached the outside of the club, climbed into the rear seat of a

They Are Ruining Ibiza

taxi, and lay motionless while the driver attempted to get a destination from him.

"Santa Eulalia," Charles struggled upright, "Santa Eulalia, *por favor. Hotel Ses Estaques.*"

The driver looked toward the doorway where Susan still struggled to leave, "*Y la mama desnudo?*"

Charles looked back, and muttered in English, "The nude mama stays behind."

The driver started the motor but did not move. "*Mil seiscientas pesetas; comprende, Vd., señor?*"

Charles nodded wearily, "*Yo comprendo* . . . sixteen hundred *pesetas*, in *ingles*. Every destination in life's sixteen hundred fucking *pesetas*."

"*Sí* . . . *'sta bien!* Okay," the driver gave an Ibicenco smile with many teeth, but Charles had closed his eyes.

Eight

There were few lights on either side of the highway. Occasionally they passed another club and the driver pronounced the names aloud, as if giving a tour: "Pasha," he exclaimed, then a little further, "Pliygorl" then "Nikki's."

"Fuck Nikki . . . fuck them all," Charles said.

The driver agreed, "Fuuk tham all."

They Are Ruining Ibiza

Charles added, with more emphasis, "Fuck *todo el mundo*," and the driver again agreed solemnly, "Fuuk *todo el mundo*." Charles said bitterly, "They're ruining Ibiza," and the driver replied bitterly, "*Sí* . . . thay ar' rrruining Ibiza."

With that, Charles slumped onto the cool leather of the taxi's seat and passed out. Later, as the taxi turned off the highway onto the private road toward the hotel, he came awake and said to the driver, "*Señor, alto, por favor.* Stop here. *Aquí.*"

The driver stopped the cab but asked, "*Aquí? Pero, el hotel no es aquí.*"

"I'll walk . . . *doy un paseo*, or whatever th' hell . . . got to clear my head. *Tonto de cabeza, comprende?* Crazy in the head." The driver answered, good-naturedly, "*Sí, tonto de cabeza.*"

Charles attempted to count the *pesetas* but gave up and held out a handful to the driver. The driver looked at the money, then at Charles. "*Cuantos?*"

"Take it all," Charles said, "Take *todos dineros* . . . "

The driver counted the money and bowed his head at Charles, "*Gracias . . . mil gracias.*"

Charles told the driver, solemnly, "They are ruining Ibiza."

The driver answered solemnly, "*Sí,* thay ar' rrruining Ibiza."

When Charles got out, the taxi remained, its lights illuminating the gravel road so that Charles could find his

119

A. C. Greene

way. He turned and waved at the lights, making the universal sign of acceptance. The taxi backed around and disappeared toward Santa Eulalia.

❁❁❁❁

He stumbled along the dark road, "*Tonto de cabeza . . . tonto de cabeza . . .*" singing in his head, telling him he was a fool. "Shut up," he growled back at the words. The dark road led along the inner harbor, passing the foot of the jetty being built for the Senator. From across the water of the bay he heard music, the universal thump, thump he had left at Club *¿Cual?*

"What the hell is that?" he said, and changed paths, leaving the road to the hotel to go stumble along the jetty. "Be goddamn!" The music was coming from the yacht with the Texas flag.

He walked unsteadily along the jetty until he was able to see life aboard the boat, catch the laughter and loud but wordless voices.

"Fucking barbarians," he growled to himself, then yelled at the yacht. "You sons of bitches!"

The words disappeared over the water, and he began running at a stagger along the dirt road of the unfinished jetty. Suddenly he heard a truck groaning up the slope, coming toward him; terror drove him to a lurching jog and, just ahead came the thump and splash of the boulders as the crane clawed them from the vehicles and let

They Are Ruining Ibiza

them drop, inexorably, into the bay. He was panting desperately, trapped—but as suddenly as it began, the noise stopped. He looked around frantically. No trucks were near; the crane, its tall boom lowered, perched remotely far, in the dark at the end of the jetty. "God! I'm going crazy . . . *tonto de cabeza.*"

But the music grew louder, driving out the memory of the trucks, the crane, the splashing boulders; pushing through the frenzied darkness to surround him. The laughter from the yacht became distinct, and his heightened awareness intensified the sound of glasses clinking, of voices lilting or deep, male and female; shadows moved across the portholes of the boat, but no one was evident . . . only the music, the sounds of gaiety and party laughter. He came as near the yacht as he could on the jetty. The sounds coming ashore, like heedless waves, were indifferent to his presence, taunting him with their indifference, and he began screaming: "Goddamn you . . . you're ruining Ibiza!" The music pounded his ears while the human sounds continued in a bright unintelligible stream which penetrated his head, piercing behind his eyes to create slivers of glass-sharp pain.

He yelled, his voice hoarse, "You're ruining the world . . . th' whole goddamn world!"

Nothing happened, no sound was added or subtracted. He felt along the roadway at his feet and found a rock the size of his fist. He pulled back his arm, aiming carefully, and threw the rock directly at the yacht. He heard the rock splash harmlessly in the water of the bay. He found a second rock and, with even greater care, hurled it as hard as he could. It, too, splashed in the bay. "Shit . . . shit!" Screaming again, he threw another rock, and another, his right shoulder burning from the unfamiliar exertion, and they, too, splashed into the bay.

Suddenly a million-candlepower spotlight beamed directly at him, came on from the yacht, blinding him. He fell back, shaking his fists, "You're ruining Ibiza . . . don't you care? You are ruining the world! The goddamn world!" The loud rock music continued. Then, crying and cursing, he began scrambling for rocks, sticks, dirt—anything—and started madly throwing and shoveling the debris with his hands in the direction of the yacht. He toiled in the blinding white of the spotlight, shaking his head frantically, searching the jetty for missiles but not turning to see where they might land, tossing without aiming. He stood panting, his hands shaking and bleeding from the sharp-edged rocks, his face twitching uncontrollably. "*Todo el mundo,*" he screamed, "*todo el mundo . . .*" He could not see now, the terrible whiteness of the spotlight cracking his eyes, penetrating his skull, his mind as he was babbling and weeping, ". . . ruining Ibiza . . . ruining . . . everything."

The spotlight went out; darkness was thick and sudden. The world on the jetty was inky and isolated again. The music continued, the figures on the yacht, like shadows on a screen, were dancing, laughing, the

They Are Ruining Ibiza

clink of glass and bottle punctuating the laughter. Now and then a voice was lifted, but words were never audible. Dr. Charles Martyn, sobbing, sat on the dirt path of the jetty in the dark alone, reaching now and then for a pebble, a handful of dirt, sobbing and muttering, "They are ruining Ibiza . . . ruining everything . . . ruining the whole damn world . . . ."